Heinrich Böll: *18 Stories*

1

HEINRICH BÖLL
18 STORIES

Translated from the German by Leila Vennewitz

 McGraw-Hill Book Company

New York • St. Louis • San Francisco • Düsseldorf • Kuala Lumpur

Mexico • Montreal • Panama • Rio de Janeiro • Sydney • Toronto

Library of Congress Catalog Card Number: 66-23273

First McGraw-Hill Paperback Edition, 1971

07-006416-4

5678910 MUMU 7654

Translator's Acknowledgment

I am deeply indebted to my husband, William, for his assistance in this translation.

Leila Vennewitz

Vancouver, Canada

Contents

Heinrich Böll: *18 Stories*

Like a bad dream

That evening we had invited the Zumpens over for dinner, nice people; it was through my father-in-law that we
had got to know them: ever since we have been married
he has helped me to meet people who can be useful to me
in business, and Zumpen can be useful: he is chairman
of a committee which places contracts for large housing
projects, and I have married into the excavating business.

I was tense that evening, but Bertha, my wife, reassured me. "The fact," she said, "that he's coming at
all is promising. Just try and get the conversation round
to the contract. You know it's tomorrow they're going to
be awarded."

I stood looking through the net curtains of the glass
front door, waiting for Zumpen. I smoked, ground the
cigarette butts under my foot, and shoved them under
the mat. Next I took up a position at the bathroom window and stood there wondering why Zumpen had accepted the invitation; he couldn't be that interested in
having dinner with us, and the fact that the big contract I

was involved in was going to be awarded tomorrow must have made the whole thing as embarrassing to him as it was to me.

I thought about the contract too: it was a big one, I would make 20,000 marks on the deal, and I wanted the money.

Bertha had decided what I was to wear: a dark jacket, trousers a shade lighter and a conservative tie. That's the kind of thing she learned at home, and at boarding school from the nuns. Also what to offer guests: when to pass the cognac, and when the vermouth, how to arrange dessert. It is comforting to have a wife who knows all about such things.

But Bertha was tense too: as she put her hands on my shoulders, they touched my neck, and I felt her thumbs damp and cold against it.

"It's going to be all right," she said, "You'll get the contract."

"Christ," I said, "it means 20,000 marks to me, and you know how we need the money."

"One should never," she said gently, "mention Christ's name in connection with money!"

A dark car drew up in front of our house, a make I didn't recognize, but it looked Italian. "Take it easy," Bertha whispered, "wait till they've rung, let them stand there for a couple of seconds, then walk slowly to the door and open it."

I watched Mr. and Mrs. Zumpen come up the steps: he is slender and tall, with graying temples, the kind of man who fifty years ago would have been known as a "ladies' man"; Mrs. Zumpen is one of those thin dark women who always make me think of lemons. I could tell from Zumpen's face that it was a frightful bore for him to have dinner with us.

Then the doorbell rang, and I waited one second, two seconds, walked slowly to the door and opened it.

"Well," I said, "how nice of you to come!"

Cognac glasses in hand, we went from room to room in our apartment, which the Zumpens wanted to see. Bertha stayed in the kitchen to squeeze some mayonnaise out of a tube onto the appetizers; she does this very nicely: hearts, loops, little houses. The Zumpens complimented us on our apartment; they exchanged smiles when they saw the big desk in my study, at that moment it seemed a bit too big even to me.

Zumpen admired a small rococo cabinet, a wedding present from my grandmother, and a baroque Madonna in our bedroom.

By the time we got back to the dining room, Bertha had dinner on the table; she had done this very nicely too, it was all so attractive yet so natural, and dinner was pleasant and relaxed. We talked about movies and books, about the recent elections, and Zumpen praised the assortment of cheeses, and Mrs. Zumpen praised the coffee and the pastries. Then we showed the Zumpens our honeymoon pictures: photographs of the Breton coast, Spanish donkeys, and street scenes from Casablanca.

After that we had some more cognac, and when I stood up to get the box with the photos of the time when we were engaged, Bertha gave me a sign, and I didn't get

the box. For two minutes there was absolute silence, because we had nothing more to talk about, and we all
thought about the contract; I thought of the 20,000
marks, and it struck me that I could deduct the bottle of
cognac from my income tax. Zumpen looked at his
watch and said: "Too bad, it's ten o'clock; we have to
go. It's been such a pleasant evening!" And Mrs. Zumpen said: "It was really delightful, and I hope you'll
come to us one evening."

"We would love to," Bertha said, and we stood
around for another half-minute, all thinking again about
the contract, and I felt Zumpen was waiting for me to
take him aside and bring up the subject. But I didn't.
Zumpen kissed Bertha's hand, and I went ahead, opened
the doors, and held the car door open for Mrs. Zumpen
down below.

"Why," said Bertha gently, "didn't you mention the
contract to him? You know it's going to be awarded tomorrow."

"Well," I said, "I didn't know how to bring the conversation round to it."

"Now look," she said in a quiet voice, "you could
have used any excuse to ask him into your study, that's
where you should have talked to him. You must have noticed how interested he is in art. You ought to have said:
I have an eighteenth-century crucifix in there you might
like to have a look at, and then . . ."

I said nothing, and she sighed and tied on her apron.
I followed her into the kitchen; we put the rest of the ap-

petizers back in the refrigerator, and I crawled about on the floor looking for the top of the mayonnaise tube. I put away the remains of the cognac, counted the cigars: Zumpen had smoked only one. I emptied the ashtrays, ate another pastry, and looked to see if there was any coffee left in the pot. When I went back to the kitchen, Bertha was standing there with the car key in her hand.

"What's up?" I asked.

"We have to go over there, of course," she said.

"Over where?"

"To the Zumpens," she said, "where do you think?"

"It's nearly half past ten."

"I don't care if it's midnight," Bertha said, "all I know is, there's 20,000 marks involved. Don't imagine they're squeamish."

She went into the bathroom to get ready, and I stood behind her watching her wipe her mouth and draw in new outlines, and for the first time I noticed how wide and primitive that mouth is. When she tightened the knot of my tie I could have kissed her, the way I always used to when she fixed my tie, but I didn't.

Downtown the cafés and restaurants were brightly lit. People were sitting outside on the terraces, and the light from the street lamps was caught in the silver ice-cream dishes and ice buckets. Bertha gave me an encouraging look; but she stayed in the car when we stopped in front of the Zumpens' house, and I pressed the bell at once and was surprised how quickly the door was opened. Mrs. Zumpen did not seem surprised to see me; she had on some black lounging pajamas with loose full trousers embroidered with yellow flowers, and this made me think more than ever of lemons.

"I beg your pardon," I said, "I would like to speak to your husband."

"He's gone out again," she said, "he'll be back in half an hour."

In the hall I saw a lot of Madonnas, gothic and baroque, even rococo Madonnas, if there is such a thing.

"I see," I said, "well then, if you don't mind, I'll come back in half an hour."

Bertha had bought an evening paper; she was reading it and smoking, and when I sat down beside her she said: "I think you could have talked about it to her too."

"But how do you know he wasn't there?"

"Because I know he is at the Gaffel Club playing chess, as he does every Wednesday evening at this time."

"You might have told me that earlier."

"Please try and understand," said Bertha, folding the newspaper. "I am trying to help you, I want you to find out for yourself how to deal with such things. All we had to do was call up Father and he would have settled the whole thing for you with one phone call, but I want you to get the contract on your own."

"All right," I said, "then what'll we do: wait here half an hour, or go up right away and have a talk with her?"

"We'd better go up right away," said Bertha.

We got out of the car and went up in the elevator together. "Life," said Bertha, "consists of making compromises and concessions."

Mrs. Zumpen was no more surprised now than she had been earlier, when I had come alone. She greeted us, and we followed her into her husband's study. Mrs. Zumpen brought some cognac, poured it out, and before I could say anything about the contract she pushed a yellow folder toward me: "Housing Project Fir Tree Haven," I read, and looked up in alarm at Mrs. Zumpen, at Bertha, but they both smiled, and Mrs. Zumpen said: "Open the folder," and I opened it; inside was another one, pink, and on this I read: "Housing Project Fir Tree Haven—Excavation Work." I opened this too, saw my estimate lying there on top of the pile; along the upper edge someone had written in red: "Lowest bid."

I could feel myself flushing with pleasure, my heart thumping, and I thought of the 20,000 marks.

"Christ," I said softly, and closed the file, and this time Bertha forgot to rebuke me.

"*Prost,*" said Mrs. Zumpen with a smile, "let's drink to it then."

We drank, and I stood up and said: "It may seem rude of me, but perhaps you'll understand that I would like to go home now."

"I understand perfectly," said Mrs. Zumpen, "there's just one small item to be taken care of." She took the file, leafed through it, and said: "Your price per square meter is thirty pfennigs below that of the next-lowest bidder. I suggest you raise your price by fifteen pfennigs: that way you'll still be the lowest and you'll have made an extra four thousand five hundred marks. Come on, do it now!" Bertha took her pen out of her purse and offered it to me, but I was in too much of a turmoil to write; I gave the file to Bertha and watched her alter the price with a steady hand, re-write the total, and hand the file back to Mrs. Zumpen.

"And now," said Mrs. Zumpen, "just one more little thing. Get out your check book and write a check for three thousand marks; it must be a cash check and endorsed by you."

She had said this to me, but it was Bertha who pulled our check book out of her purse and made out the check.

"It won't be covered," I said in a low voice.

"When the contract is awarded, there will be an advance, and then it will be covered," said Mrs. Zumpen.

Perhaps I failed to grasp what was happening at the time. As we went down in the elevator, Bertha said she was happy, but I said nothing.

Bertha chose a different way home, we drove through quiet residential districts, I saw lights in open windows, people sitting on balconies drinking wine; it was a clear, warm night.

"I suppose the check was for Zumpen?" was all I said, softly, and Bertha replied, just as softly: "Of course."

I looked at Bertha's small, brown hands on the steering wheel, so confident and quiet. Hands, I thought, that sign checks and squeeze mayonnaise tubes, and I looked higher—at her mouth, and still felt no desire to kiss it.

That evening I did not help Bertha put the car away in the garage, nor did I help her with the dishes. I poured myself a large cognac, went up to my study, and sat down at my desk, which was much too big for me. I was wondering about something. I got up, went into the bedroom and looked at the baroque Madonna, but even there I couldn't put my finger on the thing I was wondering about.

The ringing of the phone interrupted my thoughts; I lifted the receiver and was not surprised to hear Zumpen's voice.

"Your wife," he said, "made a slight mistake. She raised the price by twenty-five pfennigs instead of fifteen."

I thought for a moment and then said: "That wasn't a mistake, she did it with my consent."

He was silent for a second or two, then said with a laugh: "So you had already discussed the various possibilities?"

"Yes," I said.

"All right, then make out another check for a thousand."

"Five hundred," I said, and I thought: It's like a bad dream—that's what it's like.

"Eight hundred," he said, and I said with a laugh: "Six hundred," and I knew, although I had no experience to go on, that he would now say seven hundred and fifty, and when he did I said "Yes" and hung up.

It was not yet midnight when I went downstairs and over to the car to give Zumpen the check; he was alone and laughed as I reached in to hand him the folded check. When I walked slowly back into the house, there was no sign of Bertha; she didn't appear when I went back into my study; she didn't appear when I went downstairs again for a glass of milk from the refrigerator, and I knew what she was thinking; she was thinking: he has to get over it, and I have to leave him alone; this is something he has to understand.

But I never did understand. It is beyond understanding.

The thrower-away

For the last few weeks I have been trying to avoid people who might ask me what I do for a living. If I really had to put a name to my occupation, I would be forced to utter a word which would alarm people. So I prefer the abstract method of putting down my confession on paper.

Until recently I would have been prepared at any time to make an oral confession. I almost insisted. I called myself an inventor, a scholar, even a student, and, in the melodramatic mood of incipient intoxication, an unrecognized genius. I basked in the cheerful fame which a frayed collar can radiate; arrogantly, as if it were mine by right, I exacted reluctant credit from suspicious shopkeepers who watched margarine, ersatz coffee and cheap tobacco disappear into my pockets; I reveled in my unkempt appearance, and at breakfast, lunch and dinner I drank the nectar of Bohemian life: the bliss of knowing one is not conforming.

But for the past few weeks I have been boarding the streetcar every morning just before 7:30 at the corner of the Roonstrasse; like everyone else I meekly hold out my season ticket to the conductor. I have on a gray double-breasted suit, a striped shirt, a dark-green tie, I carry my sandwiches in a flat aluminum box and hold the morning paper, lightly rolled, in my hand. I look like a citizen who has managed to avoid introspection. After the third stop I get up to offer my seat to one of the elderly working women who have got on at the housing settlement. Having sacrificed my seat on the altar of social compassion, I continue to read the newspaper standing up, now and again letting myself be heard in the capacity of arbitrator when morning irritation is inclined to make people unjust. I correct the worst political and historical errors (by explaining, for instance, that there is a certain difference between SA and USA); as soon as anyone puts a cigarette to his lips I discreetly hold my lighter in front of his nose and, with the aid of the tiny but dependable flame, light his morning cigarette for him. Thus I complete the picture of a well-groomed fellow-citizen who is still young enough for people to say he "has nice manners."

I seem to have been successful in donning the mask which makes it impossible to ask me about my occupation. I am evidently taken for an educated businessman dealing in attractively packaged and agreeably smelling articles such as coffee, tea or spices, or in valuable small objects which are pleasing to the eye such as jewelry or watches; a man who practices his profession in a nice old-fashioned office with dark oil paintings of merchant forebears hanging on the walls, who phones his wife

about ten, who knows how to imbue his apparently impassive voice with that hint of tenderness which betrays
affection and concern. Since I also participate in the
usual jokes and do not refrain from laughing when
every morning at the Lohengrinstrasse the clerk from
City Hall shouts out "When does the next swan leave?",
since I do not withhold my comments concerning either
the events of the day or the results of the football pools,
I am obviously regarded as someone who, although
prosperous (as can be seen from his suit material), has
an attitude toward life which is deeply rooted in the
principles of democracy. An air of integrity encases me
the way the glass coffin encased Snow White.

When a passing truck provides the streetcar window
with a background for a moment, I check up on the expression on my face: isn't it perhaps rather too pensive,
almost verging on the sorrowful? I assiduously erase the
remnants of brooding and do my best to give my face the
expression I want it to wear: neither reserved nor familiar, neither superficial nor profound.

My camouflage seems to be successful, for when I get
out at the Marienplatz and dive into the maze of streets
in the Old Town, where there is no lack of nice old-
fashioned offices, where notaries and lawyers abound, no
one suspects that I pass through a rear entrance into the
UBIA building—a firm that can boast of supporting
350 people and of insuring the lives of 400,000. The
commissionaire greets me with a smile at the delivery
entrance, I walk past him, go down to the basement, and
start in on my work, which has to be completed by the

time the employees come pouring into the offices at 8:30. The activity that I pursue every morning between 8 and 8:30 in the basement of this respected establishment is devoted entirely to destruction. I throw away.

It took me years to invent my profession, to endow it with mathematical plausibility. I wrote treatises; graphs and charts covered—and still cover—the walls of my apartment. For years I climbed along abscissas and up ordinates, wallowed in theories, and savored the glacial ecstasy of solving formulas. Yet since practicing my profession and seeing my theories come to life, I am filled with a sense of sadness such as may come over a general who finds himself obliged to descend from the heights of strategy to the plains of tactics.

I enter my workroom, exchange my jacket for a gray smock, and immediately set to work. I open the mailbags which the commissionaire has already picked up earlier from the main post office, and I empty them into the two wooden bins which, constructed according to my design, hang to the right and left on the wall over my worktable. This way I only need to stretch out my hands, somewhat like a swimmer, and begin swiftly to sort the mail.

First I separate the circulars from the letters, a purely routine job, since a glance at the postage suffices. At this stage a knowledge of the postal tariff renders hesitation unnecessary. After years of practice I am able to complete this phase within half an hour, and by this time it is half past eight and I can hear the footsteps of the employees pouring into the offices overhead. I ring for the commissionaire, who takes the sorted letters to the vari-

ous departments. It never fails to sadden me, the sight of
the commissionaire carrying off in a metal tray the size
of a briefcase the remains of what had once filled three
mailbags. I might feel triumphant, for this, the vindica-
tion of my theory of throwing away, has for years been
the objective of my private research; but, strangely
enough, I do not feel triumphant. To have been right is
by no means always a reason for rejoicing.

After the departure of the commissionaire there remains the task of examining the huge pile of printed
matter to make sure it contains no letter masquerading
behind the wrong postage, no bill mailed as a circular.
This work is almost always superfluous, for the probity
of the mailing public is nothing short of astounding. I
must admit that here my calculations were incorrect: I
had overestimated the number of postal defrauders.

Rarely has a post card, a letter or a bill sent as printed
matter escaped my notice; about half past nine I ring for
the commissionaire, who takes the remaining objects of
my careful scrutiny to the departments.

The time has now come when I require some refreshment. The commissionaire's wife brings me my coffee, I
take my sandwich out of the flat aluminum box, sit down
for my break, and chat with the commissionaire's wife
about her children. Is Alfred doing somewhat better in
arithmetic? Has Gertrude been able to catch up in spelling? Alfred is not doing any better in arithmetic, whereas Gertrude has been able to catch up in spelling. Have
the tomatoes ripened properly, are the rabbits plump,
and was the experiment with the melons successful? The

tomatoes have not ripened properly, but the rabbits are plump, while the experiment with the melons is still undecided. Serious problems, such as whether one should stock up on potatoes or not, matters of education, such as whether one should enlighten one's children or be enlightened by them, are the subjects of our intense consideration.

Just before eleven the commissionaire's wife leaves, and usually she asks me to let her have some travel folders. She is collecting them, and I smile at her enthusiasm, for I have retained tender memories of travel folders. As a child I also collected travel folders, I used to fish them out of my father's waste-paper basket. Even as a boy it bothered me that my father would take mail from the mailman and throw it into the waste-paper basket without looking at it. This action wounded my innate propensity for economy: there was something that had been designed, set up, printed, put in an envelope, and stamped, that had passed through the mysterious channels by which the postal service actually causes our mail to arrive at our addresses; it was weighted with the sweat of the draftsman, the writer, the printer, the office boy who had stuck on the stamps; on various levels and in various tariffs it had cost money: all this only to end —without being deemed worthy of so much as a glance —in a waste-paper basket?

At the age of eleven I had already adopted the habit of taking out of the waste-paper basket, as soon as my father had left for the office, whatever had been thrown away. I would study it, sort it, and put it away in a chest which I used to keep toys in. Thus by the time I was twelve I already possessed an imposing collection of wine-merchants' catalogues, as well as prospectuses on naturopathy and natural history. My collection of travel folders assumed the dimensions of a geographical encyclopedia; Dalmatia was as familiar to me as the Norwegian fjords, Scotland as close as Zakopane, the forests of Bohemia soothed me while the waves of the Atlantic disquieted me; hinges were offered me, houses and buttons, political parties asked for my vote, charities for my money; lotteries promised me riches, religious sects poverty. I leave it to the reader's imagination to picture what my collection was like when at the age of seventeen, suddenly bored with it all, I offered my collection to a junk dealer who paid me 7 marks and 60 pfennigs for it.

Having finished school, I embarked in my father's footsteps and set my foot on the first rung of the civil service ladder. With the 7 marks and 60 pfennigs I bought a package of squared paper and three colored crayons, and my attempt to gain a foothold in the civil service turned into a laborious detour, for a happy thrower-away was slumbering in me while I filled the role of an unhappy junior clerk. All my free time was devoted to intricate calculations.

Stop-watch, pencil, slide-rule, squared paper, these were the props of my obsession; I calculated how long it took to open a circular of small, medium or large size, with or without pictures, give it a quick glance, satisfy oneself of its uselessness, and then throw it in the waste-paper basket, a process requiring a minimum of five sec-onds and a maximum of twenty-five; if the circular is at all attractive, either the text or the pictures, several min-utes, often a quarter of an hour, must be allowed for this. By conducting bogus negotiations with printing firms, I also worked out the minimum production costs for circulars. Indefatigably I checked the results of my studies and adjusted them (it did not occur to me until two years later that the time of the cleaning-women who have to empty the waste-paper baskets had to be in-cluded in my calculations); I applied the results of my research to firms with ten, twenty, a hundred or more employees; and I arrived at results which an expert on economics would not have hesitated to describe as alarming.

Obeying my sense of loyalty, I began by offering my results to my superiors; although I had reckoned with the possibility of ingratitude, I was nevertheless shocked at the extent of that ingratitude. I was accused of neg-lecting my duties, suspected of nihilism, pronounced "a mental case," and discharged. To the great sorrow of my kind parents, I abandoned my promising career, began new ones, broke these off too, forsook the warmth of the parental hearth, and, as I have already said, eked out my existence as an unrecognized genius. I took pleasure in the humiliation of vainly peddling my invention, and spent years in a blissful state of being anti-social, so consistently that my punch-card in the central files which had long ago been punched with the symbol for "mental case" was now stamped with the confidential symbol for "antisocial."

In view of these circumstances, it can readily be imagined what a shock it was when the obviousness of my results at last became obvious to someone else—the manager of UBIA, how deeply humiliated I was to have to wear a dark-green tie, yet I must continue to go around in disguise as I am terrified of being found out. I try anxiously to give my face the proper expression when I laugh at the Lohengrin joke, since there is no greater vanity than that of the wags who populate the streetcar every morning. Sometimes, too, I am afraid the streetcar may be full of people who the previous day have done work which I am about to destroy that very morning: printers, typesetters, draftsmen, writers who compose the wording of advertisements, commercial artists, envelope stuffers, packers, apprentices of all kinds. From 8 to 8:30 every morning I ruthlessly destroy the products of respected paper mills, worthy printing establishments, brilliant commercial artists, the texts of talented writers; coated paper, glossy paper, copperplate, I take it all, just as it comes from the mailbag, and without the faintest sentimentality tie it up into handy bundles for the waste-paper dealer. In the space of one hour I destroy the output of 200 work-hours and save UBIA a further 100 hours, so that altogether (here I must lapse into my own jargon) I achieve a concentrate of 1:300.

When the commissionaire's wife leaves with the empty coffeepot and the travel folders, I knock off. I wash my hands, exchange my smock for my jacket, pick up the morning paper, and leave the UBIA building by the rear entrance. I stroll through the town and wonder how I can escape from tactics and get back into strategy. That which intoxicated me as a formula, I find disappointing, since it can be performed so easily. Strategy translated into action can be carried out by hacks. I shall probably establish schools for throwers-away. I may possibly also attempt to have throwers-away placed in post offices, perhaps even in printing establishments; an enormous amount of energy, valuable commodities, and intelligence could be utilized as well as postage saved; it might even be feasible to conceive, compose, and set brochures up in type but not print them. These are all problems still requiring a lot of study.

However, the mere throwing away of mail as such has almost ceased to interest me; any improvements on that level can be worked out by means of the basic formula. For a long time now I have been devoting my attention to calculations concerning wrapping paper and the process of wrapping: this is virgin territory where nothing has been done, here one can strive to spare humanity those unprofitable efforts under the burden of which it is groaning. Every day billions of throwing-away movements are made, energies are dissipated which, could they but be utilized, would suffice to change the face of the earth. It would be a great advantage if one were permitted to undertake experiments in department stores; should one dispense with the wrapping process altogether, or should one post an expert thrower-away right next to the wrapping table who unwraps what has just been wrapped and immediately ties the wrapping paper into bundles for the waste-paper dealer? These are problems meriting some thought. In any case it has struck me that in many shops the customers implore the clerk not to wrap the purchased article, but that they have to submit to having it wrapped. Clinics for nervous diseases are rapidly filling with patients who complain of an attack of nerves whenever they unwrap a bottle of perfume or a box of chocolates, or open a packet of cigarettes, and at the moment I am making an intensive study of a young man from my neighborhood who earned his living as a book reviewer but at times was unable to practice his profession because he found it impossible to undo the twisted wire tied around the parcel, and even when he did find himself equal to this physical exertion, he was incapable of penetrating the massive layer of gummed paper with which the corrugated paper is stuck together. The man appears deeply disturbed and has now gone over to reviewing the books unread and placing the parcels on his bookshelves without unwrapping them. I leave it to the reader's imagination to depict for himself the effect of such a case on our intellectual life.

While walking through the town between eleven and one I observe all sorts of details: I spend some time unobtrusively in the department stores, hovering around the wrapping tables; I stand in front of tobacco shops and pharmacies and note down minor statistics; now and again I even purchase something, so as to allow the senseless procedure to be performed on myself and to discover how much effort is required actually to take possession of the article one wishes to own.

So between eleven and one in my impeccable suit I complete the picture of a man who is sufficiently prosperous to afford a bit of leisure—who at about one o'clock enters a sophisticated little restaurant, casually chooses the most expensive meal, and scribbles some hieroglyphics on his beer coaster which could equally well be stock quotations or flights of poetry; who knows how to praise or decry the quality of the meat with arguments which betray the connoisseur to even the most blasé waiter; who, when it comes to choosing dessert, hesitates with a knowing air between cake, ice cream and cheese; and who finishes off his scribblings with a flourish which proves that they were stock quotations after all.

Shocked at the results of my calculations I leave the little restaurant. My expression becomes more and more thoughtful while I search for a small café where I can pass the time till three o'clock and read the evening paper. At three I re-enter the UBIA building by the rear door to take care of the afternoon mail, which consists almost exclusively of circulars. It is a matter of scarcely fifteen minutes to pick out the ten or twelve letters; I don't even have to wash my hands after it, I just brush them off, take the letters to the commissionaire, leave the building, and at the Marienplatz board the streetcar, glad that on the way home I do not need to laugh at the Lohengrin joke. When the dark tarpaulin of a passing truck makes a background for the streetcar window, I can see my face: it is relaxed; that is to say pensive, almost brooding, and I relish the fact that I do not have to put on any other face, for at this hour none of my morning fellow-travelers has finished work. I get out at the Roonstrasse, buy some fresh rolls, a piece of cheese or sausage, some ground coffee, and walk up to my little apartment, the walls of which are hung with graphs and charts, with hectic curves: between the abscissas and ordinates I capture the lines of a fever going up and up; not a single one of my curves goes down, not a single one of my formulas has the power to soothe me. I groan under the burden of my vision of economics, and while the water is boiling for the coffee I place my slide-rule, my notes, pencil and paper in readiness.

My apartment is sparsely furnished, it looks more like a laboratory. I drink my coffee standing up and hastily swallow a sandwich, the epicure I was at noon is now a thing of the past. Wash hands, light a cigarette, then I set my stop-watch and unwrap the nerve tonic I bought that morning on my stroll through the town: outer wrapping paper, cellophane covering, carton, inside wrapping paper, directions for use secured by a rubber band: thirty-seven seconds. The nervous energy consumed in unwrapping exceeds the nervous energy which the tonic promises to impart to me, but there may be subjective reasons for this which I shall disregard in my calculations. One thing is certain: the wrapping is worth more than the contents, and the cost of the twenty-five yellow tablets is out of all proportion to their value. But these are considerations verging on the moral aspect, and I would prefer to keep away from morality altogether. My field of speculation is one of pure economics.

Numerous articles are waiting to be unwrapped by me, many slips of paper are waiting to be evaluated; green, red, blue ink, everything is ready. It is usually late by the time I get to bed, and as I fall asleep I am haunted by my formulas, whole worlds of useless paper roll over me; some formulas explode like dynamite, the noise of the explosion sounds like a burst of laughter: it is my own, my laughter at the Lohengrin joke originating in my fear of the clerk from City Hall. Perhaps he has access to the punch-card file, has picked out my card, discovered that it contains not only the symbol for "mental case" but the second, more dangerous one for "antisocial." There is nothing more difficult to fill than a tiny hole like that in a punch-card; perhaps my laughter at the Lohengrin joke is the price I have to pay for my anonymity. I would not like to admit face to face what I find easier to do in writing: that I am a thrower-away.

The Balek scales

Where my grandfather came from, most of the people lived by working in the flax sheds. For five generations they had been breathing in the dust which rose from the crushed flax stalks, letting themselves be killed off by slow degrees, a race of long-suffering, cheerful people who ate goat cheese, potatoes, and now and then a rabbit; in the evening they would sit at home spinning and knitting; they sang, drank mint tea and were happy. During the day they would carry the flax stalks to the antiquated machines, with no protection from the dust and at the mercy of the heat which came pouring out of the drying kilns. Each cottage contained only one bed, standing against the wall like a closet and reserved for the parents, while the children slept all round the room on benches. In the morning the room would be filled with the odor of thin soup; on Sundays there was stew, and on feast days the children's faces would light up with pleasure as they watched the black acorn coffee turning paler and paler from the milk their smiling mother poured into their coffee mugs.

The parents went off early to the flax sheds, the housework was left to the children: they would sweep the room, tidy up, wash the dishes and peel the potatoes, precious pale-yellow fruit whose thin peel had to be produced afterwards to dispel any suspicion of extravagance or carelessness.

As soon as the children were out of school they had to go off into the woods and, depending on the season, gather mushrooms and herbs: woodruff and thyme, caraway, mint and foxglove, and in summer, when they had brought in the hay from their meager fields, they gathered hayflowers. A kilo of hayflowers was worth one pfennig, and they were sold by the apothecaries in town for twenty pfennigs a kilo to highly strung ladies. The mushrooms were highly prized: they fetched twenty pfennigs a kilo and were sold in the shops in town for one mark twenty. The children would crawl deep into the green darkness of the forest during the autumn when dampness drove the mushrooms out of the soil, and almost every family had its own places where it gathered mushrooms, places which were handed down in whispers from generation to generation.

The woods belonged to the Baleks, as well as the flax sheds, and in my grandfather's village the Baleks had a chateau, and the wife of the head of the family had a little room next to the dairy where mushrooms, herbs and hayflowers were weighed and paid for. There on the table stood the great Balek scales, an old-fashioned, ornate bronze-gilt contraption, which my grandfather's grandparents had already faced when they were children, their grubby hands holding their little baskets of mushrooms, their paper bags of hayflowers, breathlessly watching the number of weights Frau Balek had to throw on the scale before the swinging pointer came to rest exactly over the black line, that thin line of justice which had to be redrawn every year. Then Frau Balek would take the big book covered in brown leather, write down the weight, and pay out the money, pfennigs or ten-pfennig pieces and very, very occasionally, a mark. And when my grandfather was a child there was a big glass jar of lemon drops standing there, the kind that cost one mark a kilo, and when Frau Balek—whichever one happened to be presiding over the little room—was in a good mood, she would put her hand into this jar and give each child a lemon drop, and the children's faces would light up with pleasure, the way they used to when on feast days their mother poured milk into their coffee mugs, milk that made the coffee turn paler and paler until it was as pale as the flaxen pigtails of the little girls.

One of the laws imposed by the Baleks on the village was: no one was permitted to have any scales in the house. The law was so ancient that nobody gave a thought as to when and how it had arisen, and it had to be obeyed, for anyone who broke it was dismissed from the flax sheds, he could not sell his mushrooms or his thyme or his hayflowers, and the power of the Baleks was so far-reaching that no one in the neighboring villages would give him work either, or buy his forest herbs. But since the days when my grandfather's parents had gone out as small children to gather mushrooms and sell them in order that they might season the meat of the rich people of Prague or be baked into game pies, it had never occurred to anyone to break this law: flour could be measured in cups, eggs could be counted, what they had spun could be measured by the yard, and besides, the old-fashioned bronze-gilt, ornate Balek scales did not look as if there was anything wrong with them, and five generations had entrusted the swinging black pointer with what they had gone out as eager children to gather from the woods.

True, there were some among these quiet people who flouted the law, poachers bent on making more money in one night than they could earn in a whole month in the flax sheds, but even these people apparently never thought of buying scales or making their own. My grandfather was the first person bold enough to test the justice of the Baleks, the family who lived in the chateau and drove two carriages, who always maintained one boy from the village while he studied theology at the seminary in Prague, the family with whom the priest played taroc every Wednesday, on whom the local reeve, in his carriage emblazoned with the Imperial coat-of-arms, made an annual New Year's Day call and on whom the Emperor conferred a title on the first day of the year 1900.

My grandfather was hard-working and smart: he crawled further into the woods than the children of his clan had crawled before him, he penetrated as far as the thicket where, according to legend, Bilgan the Giant was supposed to dwell, guarding a treasure. But my grandfather was not afraid of Bilgan: he worked his way deep into the thicket, even when he was quite little, and brought out great quantities of mushrooms; he even found truffles, for which Frau Balek paid thirty pfennigs a pound. Everything my grandfather took to the Baleks he entered on the back of a torn-off calendar page: every pound of mushrooms, every gram of thyme, and on the right-hand side, in his childish handwriting, he entered the amount he received for each item; he scrawled in every pfennig, from the age of seven to the age of twelve, and by the time he was twelve the year 1900 had arrived, and because the Baleks had been raised to the aristocracy by the Emperor, they gave every family in the village a quarter of a pound of real coffee, the Brazilian kind; there was also free beer and tobacco for the men, and at the chateau there was a great banquet; many carriages stood in the avenue of poplars leading from the entrance gates to the chateau.

But the day before the banquet the coffee was distributed in the little room which had housed the Balek scales for almost a hundred years, and the Balek family was now called Balek von Bilgan because, according to legend, Bilgan the Giant used to have a great castle on the site of the present Balek estate.

My grandfather often used to tell me how he went there after school to fetch the coffee for four families: the Cechs, the Weidlers, the Vohlas and his own, the Brüchers. It was the afternoon of New Year's Eve: there were the front rooms to be decorated, the baking to be

done, and the families did not want to spare four boys
and have each of them go all the way to the chateau to
bring back a quarter of a pound of coffee.

And so my grandfather sat on the narrow wooden
bench in the little room while Gertrud the maid counted
out the wrapped four-ounce packages of coffee, four of
them, and he looked at the scales and saw that the pound
weight was still lying on the left-hand scale; Frau Balek
von Bilgan was busy with preparations for the banquet.
And when Gertrud was about to put her hand into the jar
with the lemon drops to give my grandfather one, she
discovered it was empty: it was refilled once a year, and
held one kilo of the kind that cost a mark.

Gertrud laughed and said: "Wait here while I get the
new lot," and my grandfather waited with the four four-
ounce packages which had been wrapped and sealed in
the factory, facing the scales on which someone had left
the pound weight, and my grandfather took the four
packages of coffee, put them on the empty scale, and his
heart thudded as he watched the black finger of justice
come to rest on the left of the black line: the scale with
the pound weight stayed down, and the pound of coffee
remained up in the air; his heart thudded more than if
he had been lying behind a bush in the forest waiting for
Bilgan the Giant, and he felt in his pocket for the pebbles he always carried with him so he could use his cata-
pult to shoot the sparrows which pecked away at his
mother's cabbage plants—he had to put three, four, five
pebbles beside the packages of coffee before the scale
with the pound weight rose and the pointer at last came

to rest over the black line. My grandfather took the coffee from the scale, wrapped the five pebbles in his kerchief, and when Gertrud came back with the big kilo bag of lemon drops which had to last for another whole year in order to make the children's faces light up with pleasure, when Gertrud let the lemon drops rattle into the glass jar, the pale little fellow was still standing there, and nothing seemed to have changed. My grandfather only took three of the packages, then Gertrud looked in startled surprise at the white-faced child who threw the lemon drop onto the floor, ground it under his heel, and said: "I want to see Frau Balek."

"Balek von Bilgan, if you please," said Gertrud.

"All right, Frau Balek von Bilgan," but Gertrud only laughed at him, and he walked back to the village in the dark, took the Cechs, the Weidlers and the Vohlas their coffee, and said he had to go and see the priest.

Instead he went out into the dark night with his five pebbles in his kerchief. He had to walk a long way before he found someone who had scales, who was permitted to have them; no one in the villages of Blaugau and Bernau had any, he knew that, and he went straight through them till, after two hours' walking, he reached the little town of Dielheim where Honig the apothecary lived. From Honig's house came the smell of fresh pancakes, and Honig's breath, when he opened the door to the half-frozen boy, already smelled of punch, there was a moist cigar between his narrow lips, and he clasped the boy's cold hands firmly for a moment, saying: "What's the matter, has your father's lung got worse?"

"No, I haven't come for medicine, I wanted . . ." My grandfather undid his kerchief, took out the five pebbles, held them out to Honig and said: "I wanted to have these weighed." He glanced anxiously into Honig's face, but when Honig said nothing and did not get angry, or even ask him anything, my grandfather said: "It is the amount that is short of justice," and now, as he went into the warm room, my grandfather realized how wet his feet were. The snow had soaked through his cheap shoes, and in the forest the branches had showered him with snow which was now melting, and he was tired and hungry and suddenly began to cry because he thought of the quantities of mushrooms, the herbs, the flowers, which had been weighed on the scales which were short five pebbles' worth of justice. And when Honig, shaking his head and holding the five pebbles, called his wife, my grandfather thought of the generations of his parents, his grandparents, who had all had to have their mushrooms, their flowers, weighed on the scales, and he was overwhelmed by a great wave of injustice, and began to sob louder than ever, and, without waiting to be asked, he sat down on a chair, ignoring the pancakes, the cup of hot coffee which nice plump Frau Honig put in front of him, and did not stop crying till Honig himself came out from the shop at the back and, rattling the pebbles in his hand, said in a low voice to his wife: "Fifty-five grams, exactly."

My grandfather walked the two hours home through the forest, got a beating at home, said nothing, not a single word, when he was asked about the coffee, spent the whole evening doing sums on the piece of paper on which he had written down everything he had sold to Frau Balek, and when midnight struck, and the cannon could be heard from the chateau, and the whole village rang with shouting and laughter and the noise of rattles, when the family kissed and embraced all round, he said into the New Year silence: "The Baleks owe me eighteen marks and thirty-two pfennigs." And again he thought of all the children there were in the village, of his brother Fritz who had gathered so many mushrooms, of his sister Ludmilla; he thought of the many hundreds of children who had all gathered mushrooms for the Baleks, and herbs and flowers, and this time he did not cry but told his parents and brothers and sisters of his discovery.

When the Baleks von Bilgan went to High Mass on New Year's Day, their new coat-of-arms—a giant crouching under a fir tree—already emblazoned in blue and gold on their carriage, they saw the hard, pale faces of the people all staring at them. They had expected garlands in the village, a song in their honor, cheers and hurrahs, but the village was completely deserted as they drove through it, and in church the pale faces of the people were turned toward them, mute and hostile, and when the priest mounted the pulpit to deliver his New Year's sermon he sensed the chill in those otherwise quiet and peaceful faces, and he stumbled painfully through his sermon and went back to the altar drenched in sweat. And as the Baleks von Bilgan left the church after Mass, they walked through a lane of mute, pale

faces. But young Frau Balek von Bilgan stopped in front
of the children's pews, sought out my grandfather's face,
pale little Franz Brücher, and asked him, right there in
the church: "Why didn't you take the coffee for your
mother?" And my grandfather stood up and said: "Because you owe me as much money as five kilos of coffee
would cost." And he pulled the five pebbles from his
pocket, held them out to the young woman and said:
"This much, fifty-five grams, is short in every pound of
your justice"; and before the woman could say anything
the men and women in the church lifted up their voices
and sang: "The justice of this earth, O Lord, hath put
Thee to death. . . ."

While the Baleks were at church, Wilhelm Vohla, the
poacher, had broken into the little room, stolen the
scales and the big fat leatherbound book in which had
been entered every kilo of mushrooms, every kilo of
hayflowers, everything bought by the Baleks in the village, and all afternoon of that New Year's Day the men
of the village sat in my great-grandparents' front room
and calculated, calculated one tenth of everything that
had been bought—but when they had calculated many
thousands of talers and had still not come to an end, the
reeve's gendarmes arrived, made their way into my great-
grandfather's front room, shooting and stabbing as they
came, and removed the scales and the book by force. My
grandfather's little sister Ludmilla lost her life, a few
men were wounded, and one of the gendarmes was
stabbed to death by Wilhelm Vohla the poacher.

Our village was not the only one to rebel: Blaugau

and Bernau did too, and for almost a week no work was done in the flax sheds. But a great many gendarmes appeared, and the men and women were threatened with prison, and the Baleks forced the priest to display the scales publicly in the school and demonstrate that the finger of justice swung to and fro accurately. And the men and women went back to the flax sheds—but no one went to the school to watch the priest: he stood there all alone, helpless and forlorn with his weights, scales, and packages of coffee.

And the children went back to gathering mushrooms, to gathering thyme, flowers and foxglove, but every Sunday, as soon as the Baleks entered the church, the hymn was struck up: "The justice of this earth, O Lord, hath put Thee to death," until the reeve ordered it proclaimed in every village that the singing of this hymn was forbidden.

My grandfather's parents had to leave the village, and the new grave of their little daughter; they became basket weavers, but did not stay long anywhere because it pained them to see how everywhere the finger of justice swung falsely. They walked along behind their cart, which crept slowly over the country roads, taking their thin goat with them, and passers-by could sometimes hear a voice from the cart singing: "The justice of this earth, O Lord, hath put Thee to death." And those who wanted to listen could hear the tale of the Baleks von Bilgan, whose justice lacked a tenth part. But there were few who listened.

My Uncle Fred

My Uncle Fred is the only person who makes my memories of the years after 1945 bearable. He came home from the war one summer afternoon, in nondescript clothes, wearing his sole possession, a tin can, on a string around his neck, and supporting the trifling weight of a few cigarette butts which he carefully saved in a little box. He embraced my mother, kissed my sister and me, mumbled something about "Bread, sleep, tobacco," and curled himself up on our family sofa, so that I remember him as being a man who was considerably longer than our sofa, a fact which obliged him either to keep his legs drawn up or let them simply hang over the end. Both alternatives moved him to rail bitterly against our grandparents' generation, to which we owed the acquisition of this valuable piece of furniture. He called these worthy people stuffy constipated owls, despised their taste for the bilious pink of the upholstery, but let none of this stop him from indulging in frequent and prolonged sleep.

I for my part was performing a thankless task in our

blameless family: I was fourteen at the time, and the sole contact with that memorable institution which we called the black market. My father had been killed in the war, my mother received a tiny pension, with the result that I had the almost daily job of peddling scraps of salvaged belongings or swapping them for bread, coal and tobacco. In those days coal was the cause of considerable violation of property rights which today we would have to bluntly call stealing. So most days saw me going out to steal or peddle, and my mother, though she realized the need for these disreputable doings, always had tears in her eyes as she watched me go off about my complicated affairs. It was my responsibility, for instance, to turn a pillow into bread, a Dresden cup into semolina, or three volumes of Gustav Freytag into two ounces of coffee, tasks to which I devoted myself with a certain amount of sporting enthusiasm but not entirely without a sense of humiliation and fear. For values—which is what grownups called them at the time—had shifted substantially, and now and then I was exposed to the unfounded suspicion of dishonesty because the value of a peddled article did not correspond in the least to the one my mother thought appropriate. It was, I must say, no pleasant task to act as broker between two different worlds of values, worlds which since then seem to have converged.

Uncle Fred's arrival led us all to expect some stalwart masculine aid. But he began by disappointing us. From the very first day I was seriously worried about his appetite, and when I made no bones about telling my mother this, she suggested I let him "find his feet." It took almost eight weeks for him to find his feet. Despite his abuse of the unsatisfactory sofa, he slept there without much trouble and spent the day dozing or describing to us in a martyred voice what position he preferred to sleep in.

I think his favorite position was that of a sprinter just before the start. He loved to lie on his back after lunch, his legs drawn up, voluptuously crumbling a large piece of bread into his mouth, and then roll himself a cigarette and sleep away the day till suppertime. He was a very tall, pale man, and there was a circular scar on his chin which gave his face somewhat the look of a damaged marble statue. Although his appetite for food and sleep continued to worry me, I liked him very much. He was the only one with whom I could at least theorize about the black market without getting into an argument. He obviously knew all about the conflict between the two worlds of values.

Although we urged him to talk to us about the war, he never did; he said it wasn't worth discussing. The only thing he would do sometimes was tell us about his induction, which seemed to have consisted chiefly of a person in uniform ordering Uncle Fred in a loud voice to urinate into a test tube, an order with which Uncle Fred was not immediately able to comply, the result being that his military career was doomed from the start. He maintained that the German Reich's keen interest in his urine had filled him with considerable distrust, a distrust which he found ominously confirmed during six years of war.

He had been a bookkeeper before the war, and when the first four weeks on our sofa had gone by, my mother suggested in her gentle sisterly way that he make inquiries about his old firm—he warily passed this suggestion on to me, but all I could discover was a pile of rubble about twenty feet high which I located in a ruined part of the city after an hour's laborious pilgrimage. Uncle Fred was much reassured by my news.

He leaned back in his chair, rolled himself a cigarette, nodded triumphantly toward my mother, and asked her to get out his old things. In one corner of our bedroom there was a carefully nailed-down crate which we opened with hammer and pliers amid much speculation; what came out of it were: twenty novels of medium size and mediocre quality, a gold pocket watch, dusty but undamaged, two pairs of suspenders, some notebooks, his Chamber of Commerce diploma, and a savings book showing a balance of twelve hundred marks. The savings book was given to me to collect the money, as well as the rest of the stuff to be peddled, including the Chamber of Commerce diploma—although this found no takers, Uncle Fred's name being inscribed on it in black India ink.

This meant that for the next four weeks we were free from worry about bread, tobacco and coal, which was a great relief to me, especially as all the schools opened wide their doors again, and I was required to complete my education.

To this day, long after my education has been completed, I have fond memories of the soups we used to get, mainly because we obtained these supplementary meals almost without a struggle, and they therefore lent a happy and contemporary note to the whole educational system.

But the outstanding event during this period was the fact that Uncle Fred finally took the initiative a good eight weeks after his safe return.

One morning in late summer he rose from his sofa, shaved so meticulously that we became apprehensive, asked for some clean underwear, borrowed my bicycle and disappeared.

His return late that night was accompanied by a great deal of noise and a penetrating smell of wine; the smell of wine emanated from my uncle's mouth, the noise was traceable to half a dozen galvanized buckets which he had tied together with some stout rope. Our confusion did not subside till we discovered he had decided to revive the flower trade in our ravaged town. My mother, full of suspicion toward the new world of values, scorned the idea, claiming that no one would want to buy flowers. But she was wrong.

It was a memorable morning when we helped Uncle Fred to take the freshly filled buckets to the streetcar stop where he set himself up in business. And I still vividly remember the sight of those red and yellow tulips, the moist carnations, nor shall I ever forget how impressive he looked as he stood there in the midst of the gray figures and piles of rubble and started calling out: "Flowers, fresh flowers—no coupons required!" I don't have to describe how his business flourished: it was a meteoric success. In a matter of four weeks he owned three dozen galvanized buckets, was the proprietor of two branches, and a month later he was paying taxes. The whole town wore a different air to me: flower stalls appeared at one street corner after another, it was impossible to keep pace with the demand; more and more buckets were procured, booths were set up and handcarts hastily thrown together.

At any rate, we were kept supplied not only with fresh flowers but with bread and coal, and I was able to retire from the brokerage business, a fact which helped greatly to improve my moral standards. For many years now, Uncle Fred has been a man of substance: his branches are still thriving, he owns a car, he looks on me as his heir, and I have been told to study commerce so I can look after the tax end of the business even before I enter on my inheritance.

When I look at him today, a solid figure behind the wheel of his red automobile, I find it strange to recall that there was really a time in my life when his appetite caused me sleepless nights.

Daniel the just

As long as it was dark the woman lying beside him could not see his face, and this made everything easier to bear. She had been talking away at him for an hour, and it did not take much effort to keep on saying "yes" or "yes of course" or "yes, that's right." The woman lying beside him was his wife, but when he thought of her he always thought: the woman. She was actually quite beautiful, and there were people who envied him his wife, and he might have had cause to be jealous—but he was not jealous; he was glad the darkness hid the sight of her face from him and allowed him to relax his own face; there was nothing more exhausting than to put on a face and wear it all day, as long as daylight lasted, and the face he showed in the daytime was a put-on face.

"If Uli doesn't make it," she said, "I can't bear to think what will happen. It would finish Marie, you know what she's gone through. Don't you?"

"Yes, of course," he said, "I know."

"She's had to eat dry bread, she—really, I don't know how she could stand it—she's slept for weeks in beds without sheets, and when Uli was born Erich was still listed as missing. If the boy doesn't get through his entrance exam—I just don't know what will happen. Don't you agree?"

"Yes, I agree," he said.

"Make sure you see the boy before he goes into the classroom where the exam's being given—say something to encourage him. You'll do what you can, won't you?"

"Yes, I will," he said.

One day in spring, thirty years ago, he too had come to town to take the entrance exam: that evening the red light of the sun had fallen over the street where his aunt lived, and to the eleven-year-old boy it seemed as if someone were spilling liquid fire over the roofs, and hundreds of windows caught this red light like molten metal.

Later, while they were sitting at supper, the windows were filled with greenish darkness for that half hour when women hesitate before turning on the light. His aunt hesitated too, and when she touched the switch she seemed to be giving the signal to hundreds and hundreds of women: suddenly yellow light from all the windows pierced the green darkness; the lights hung in the night like brittle fruits with long yellow spikes.

"Do you think you'll make it?" asked his aunt, and his uncle, who was sitting by the window holding the newspaper, shook his head as if the question were an insult.

His aunt proceeded to make up a bed for him on the bench in the kitchen, using a quilt for a mattress; his uncle let him have his blanket and his aunt one of their pillows. "You'll soon have your own bedding here," said his aunt, "and now sleep well. Good night."

"Good night," he said, and his aunt turned out the light and went into the bedroom.

His uncle stayed behind and tried to pretend he was looking for something; his hands groped across the boy's face toward the windowsill, and the hands, which smelled of wood stain and shellac, groped back across his face; his uncle's shyness hung like lead in the air, and without saying what he wanted to say he disappeared into the bedroom.

"I'll make it all right," thought the boy when he was alone, and in his mind's eye he saw his mother, who at this moment was sitting at home by the fire knitting, from time to time letting her hands fall into her lap and sending up a prayer to one of her favorite saints: Judas Thaddeus—or was Don Bosco the proper saint for him, the farm boy who had come to town to try and get into high school?

"There are some things which simply shouldn't be allowed to happen," said the woman beside him, and as she seemed to be waiting for a reply he wearily said "yes" and noticed to his despair that it was already getting light; day was coming and bringing him the hardest of all his duties: that of putting on his face.

"No," he thought, "enough things happen which shouldn't be allowed to happen." All those years ago, in the darkness on the kitchen bench, he had been so confident: he thought of the math problem, of the essay, and he was sure everything would be all right. The essay theme would almost certainly be: "A Strange Experience," and he knew exactly what he was going to describe: the visit to the institution where Uncle Thomas was confined: green and white striped chairs in the consulting room, and Uncle Thomas who—no matter what anyone said to him—always replied in the same words: "If only there were justice in this world."

"I've knitted you a lovely red pullover," said his mother, "you were always so fond of red."

"If only there were justice in this world."

They talked about the weather, about the cows and a little about politics, and Thomas always said the same thing: "If only there were justice in this world."

And later, when they walked back along the green-painted corridor, he saw at the window a thin man with narrow drooping shoulders looking mutely out into the garden.

Just before they went out through the gate, a pleasant-looking man with a kindly smile came up to them and said: "Madame, please do not forget to address me as Your Majesty," and his mother said softly to the man: "Your Majesty." And when they were standing at the streetcar stop he had looked across once more to the green house lying hidden among the trees, and seen the man with the drooping shoulders standing at the window, and a laugh rang out through the garden that sounded like tin being cut with blunt scissors.

"Your coffee's getting cold," said the woman who was his wife, "and do try and eat something at least."

He raised the coffee cup to his lips and ate something.

"I know," said the woman, laying her hand on his shoulder, "I know you're worrying about that justice of yours again, but can you call it unjust to lend a helping hand to a child? You're fond of Uli, aren't you?"

"Yes," he said, and this Yes was sincere: he was fond of Uli; the boy was sensitive, friendly and in his way intelligent, but it would be torture for him to go to high school: with a lot of extra coaching, spurred on by an ambitious mother, by dint of great effort and much intercession, he would never be more than a mediocre student. He would always have to carry the burden of a life, of demands, with which he could not cope.

"Promise me you'll do something for Uli, won't you?"

"Yes," he said, "I'll do something for him," and he kissed his wife's beautiful face and left the house. He walked slowly along, put a cigarette between his lips, dropped his put-on face and enjoyed the relaxation of feeling his own face on his skin. He looked at it in the window of a fur shop; between a gray sealskin and a leopard skin, he saw his face on the black velvet draping the display: the pale, rather puffy face of a man in his mid-forties—the face of a skeptic, a cynic perhaps; the cigarette smoke wreathed in white coils around the pale puffy face. His friend Alfred, who had died the year before, used to say: "You have never got over certain feelings of hostility—and everything you do is influenced much too much by your emotions."

Alfred had meant well, in fact what he had had in mind was right, but you can't define a person with words, and for him the word hostility was one of the most facile, one of the most convenient.

Thirty years ago, on the bench in his aunt's kitchen, he had thought: no one will write an essay like that; no one can have had such a strange experience, and before he fell asleep he thought about other things: he was going to sleep on this bench for nine years, do his homework at this table for nine years, and throughout this eternity his mother would sit at home by the fire knitting and sending up prayers to heaven. In the next room he could hear his uncle and aunt talking, and the only word he could make out from the murmuring was his name: Daniel. So they were talking about him, and although he could not make out the words he knew they were speaking kindly about him. They were fond of him, they had no children themselves. Then all of a sudden fear shot through him: in two years, he thought in panic, this bench will already be too short for me—where will I sleep then? For a few minutes this idea really scared him, but then he thought: two years, what an eternity that is, such a lot of darkness, day after day it would turn into light; and quite suddenly he slipped into that little portion of darkness which lay ahead of him—the night before the exam—and in his dreams he was pursued by the picture hanging on the wall between the buffet and the window: grim-faced men standing in front of a factory gate, one holding a tattered red flag in his hand, and in his dream the boy could clearly read the words which in the semi-darkness he had been barely able to make out: ON STRIKE.

He took leave of his face as it hung there pale and intense between the sealskin and the leopard skin in the shop window, as if drawn with a silver pencil on black cloth; he took leave reluctantly, for he saw the child he had once been, behind this face.

"On Strike," the school superintendent had said to him thirteen years later, "On Strike, do you consider that a suitable essay theme to give seventeen-year-olds?" He had not given it, and by that time, in 1934, the picture had long since disappeared from his uncle's kitchen wall. It was still possible to visit Uncle Thomas in the institution, to sit on one of the green-striped chairs, smoke cigarettes and listen to Thomas, who seemed to be replying to a litany which only he could hear: Thomas sat there listening—but he was not listening to what the visitors were saying to him, he was listening to the dirge of an invisible choir as it stood hidden in the wings of the world's stage chanting a litany to which there was but one response, Thomas's response: "If only there were justice in this world."

The man who always stood at the window looking out into the garden had one day been able—so thin had he become—to squeeze through the bars and fall headlong into the garden: his metallic laugh came crashing down with him. But His Majesty was still alive, and Heemke never failed to go up to him and whisper with a smile: "Your Majesty." "Types like that go on forever," the keeper said to him, "it'll take a lot to finish him off."

But seven years later His Majesty was no longer alive, and Thomas was dead too: they had been murdered, and the choir standing hidden in the wings of the world's stage chanting its litany waited in vain for the response which only Thomas could give.

Heemke turned into the street where the school was and he was startled to see all the candidates: they were standing around with mothers, with fathers, and over them all lay that spurious, hectic cheerfulness which descends like a sickness on people before an examination: desperate cheerfulness lay like make-up on the faces of the mothers, desperate indifference on those of the fathers.

His eye, however, was caught by a boy sitting alone and apart from the rest on the doorstep of a bombed house. Heemke stopped and felt fear rising in him like moisture in a sponge: I must watch out, he thought, if I'm not careful I'll end up sitting in Uncle Thomas's place, and maybe I'll be saying the same words. The child sitting on the doorstep reminded him of himself thirty years ago, so intensely that he felt the thirty years falling away from him like dust being blown off a statue.

Noise, laughter—the sun shone on damp roofs from which the snow had melted, and only in the shadows of the ruins was the snow still lying.

His uncle had brought him here much too early, all those years ago; they had taken the streetcar over the bridge, had not exchanged a single word, and while he was looking at the boy's black stockings he thought: shyness is a disease which deserves to be cured the way whooping cough is cured. His uncle's shyness, coupled with his own, had caught him by the throat. Mute, his red scarf round his neck, the Thermos flask in his right coat pocket, his uncle had stood beside him in the empty street, had suddenly muttered something about "go to work" and was gone, and he had sat down on a doorstep: vegetable carts rumbled over the cobbles, a baker's boy walked past with his basket of rolls, and a girl carrying a milk jug went from house to house, leaving a little blue-white spot of milk behind on every doorstep. He had been very impressed by the houses, houses in which no one seemed to be living, and today he could still see traces among the ruins of the yellow paint which had so impressed him at the time.

"Good morning, Principal," said someone walking by; he nodded briefly, and he knew that inside his colleague would say: "The old man's off his head again."

"I have three alternatives," he thought, "I can turn into that child sitting over there on the doorstep, I can go on being the man with the pale puffy face, or I can become Uncle Thomas." The alternative with the least appeal was to go on being himself: the heavy burden of carrying his put-on face. There was also not much to be said for turning into the child: books he had loved, had hated, gobbled up, devoured at the kitchen table, and every week the battle for paper, for exercise books which he filled with notes, sums, draft essays; every week thirty pfennigs which he had to fight for, till it occurred to his teacher to let him tear the blank pages out of old exercise books stored in the school basement. But he also tore out the pages where only one side had been written on, and at home he sewed them with black cotton into thick notebooks—and now he sent flowers every year for the teacher's grave in the village.

"No one," he thought, "ever knew what it cost me, not a living soul, except perhaps Alfred, but Alfred always fell back on one very silly word, hostility. It is useless to talk about it, to explain it to anyone—the last person to understand would be the one with the beautiful face who lies beside me in bed."

He hesitated a few moments longer, while the past lay upon him: what appealed to him most was to take over Uncle Thomas's role and spend his days reciting the one solitary response to the litany which the choir was chanting in the wings.

No, he didn't want to be that child again, it was too hard: what boy wears black stockings these days? The middle alternative was the one, to go on being the man with the pale puffy face, and he had always chosen the middle alternative. He walked over to the boy and as his shadow fell across him the child raised his eyes and gave him a startled look. "What's your name?" asked Heemke.

The boy got hastily to his feet and from his blushing face came the answer: "Wierzok."

"Spell it for me, please," said Heemke, reaching in his pocket for his notebook, and the child slowly spelled "W-i-e-r-z-o-k."

"And where do you come from?"

"From Wollersheim," said the child.

Thank God, thought Heemke, he's not from my village and doesn't bear my name—he's not a child of one of my many cousins.

"And where are you going to live here in town?"

"At my aunt's," said Wierzok.

"That's fine," said Heemke, "it's going to be all right with the exam. I expect you've always had good marks and a good report from your teacher, haven't you?"

"Yes, I've always had good marks."

"Don't worry," said Heemke, "it'll be all right, you will ..." He stopped, because what Alfred would have called emotion and hostility were strangling him. "Mind you don't catch a chill on those cold stones," he said in a low voice, turned on his heel and entered the school through the janitor's premises, so as to avoid Uli and Uli's mother. Concealed behind the curtain of the hall window, he looked out once more at the children and their parents waiting outside and, as happened every year on this day, he was swept by a feeling of despondency: it seemed to him that in the faces of those ten-year-old boys he could read a bleak future. They were pressing at the school gates like cattle at the stable door: among these seventy youngsters, two or three would be better than mediocre, and all the rest would simply form a background. Alfred's cynicism has penetrated me deeply, he thought, and he looked despairingly over to the Wierzok boy, who had sat down again and, his head bowed, seemed to be brooding.

When I did that I got a bad cold, thought Heemke. This boy will get through, and if I, if I—if I, what?

Hostility and emotion, Alfred my friend, these are not the words to express what I feel.

He entered the common room, greeted the other teachers who had been waiting for him, and said to the janitor who helped him off with his coat: "Have the children come in now."

He could tell from the faces of the other teachers how strange his behavior had been. "Perhaps," he thought, "I was standing out there on the street for half an hour watching the Wierzok boy," and he glanced nervously at his watch: but it was only four minutes past eight.

"Gentlemen," he said aloud, "bear in mind that for many of these children the test they are about to undergo is more crucial and decisive than university finals will be for some of them twelve years from now." They waited for more, and those who knew him were waiting for the word he was so fond of using whenever he could, the word "justice." But he said no more, merely turned to one of the teachers and quietly asked: "What is the essay theme for the candidates?"

"A Strange Experience."

Heemke stayed behind as the room emptied.

Those childish fears of his, that in two years the kitchen bench would be too short for him, had been superfluous, for he had not passed the exam although the essay theme had been "A Strange Experience." Right up to the moment when they had been let into the school he had clung to his confidence, but as soon as he entered the school his confidence had melted away.

When he came to write the essay, he tried in vain to grasp hold of Uncle Thomas. Thomas was suddenly very close, too close for him to be able to write an essay about him; he wrote down the title: "A Strange Experience," and underneath he wrote: "If only there were justice in this world," but as he wrote "justice" what he really meant was "vengeance."

It had taken him more than ten years not to think of vengeance whenever he thought of justice.

The worst of those ten years had been the year after he failed his entrance exam: the people he had left behind when he embarked on what merely seemed to promise a better life could be just as unsympathetic as those who were completely unaware, completely ignorant, and whom a phone call from his father saved from becoming involved in months of pain and effort; a smile from his mother, a clasp of the hand on Sunday after Mass, and a hasty word or two: that was the justice of this world—and the other, the thing he had always wanted but had never achieved, was what Uncle Thomas had so desperately longed for. The desire to achieve that had earned him the nickname "Daniel the Just." He was roused by the door opening, and the janitor ushered in Uli's mother.

"Marie," he said, "what—why . . ."

"Daniel," she said, "I . . . ," but he interrupted her: "I've not time now, no, not even a second," he said fiercely, and he left his room and went up to the second floor: up here the sounds of the waiting mothers were muted. He went to the window overlooking the play-ground, put a cigarette between his lips but forgot to light it. It has taken me thirty years to get over it and ar-rive at a knowledge of what it is I want. I have elimi-nated vengeance from my idea of justice; I make a good living, I put on my grim face, and most people believe this means I have reached my goal; but I have not reached my goal. I have only just begun—but now I can take off my grim face, as you put away a hat you no longer need; I shall wear a different face, perhaps my own. . . .

He would spare Wierzok this year; he did not want to make any child go through what he had gone through, any child at all, least of all this one—whom he had met as if it were himself.

The post card

None of my friends can understand the care with which I preserve a scrap of paper that has no value whatever: it merely keeps alive the memory of a certain day in my life, and to it I owe a reputation for sentimentality which is considered unworthy of my social position: I am the assistant manager of a textile firm. But I protest the accusation of sentimentality and am continually trying to invest this scrap of paper with some documentary value. It is a tiny, rectangular piece of ordinary paper, the size, but not the shape, of a stamp—it is narrower and longer than a stamp—and although it originated in the post office it has not the slightest collector's value. It has a bright red border and is divided by another red line into two rectangles of different sizes; in the smaller of these rectangles there is a big black R, in the larger one, in black print, "Düsseldorf" and a number—the number 634. That is all, and the bit of paper is yellow and thin with age, and now that I have described it minutely I have decided to throw it away: an ordinary registration sticker, such as every post office slaps on every day by the dozen.

And yet this scrap of paper reminds me of a day in my life which is truly unforgettable, although many attempts have been made to erase it from my memory. But my memory functions too well.

First of all, when I think of that day, I smell vanilla custard, a warm sweet cloud creeping under my bedroom door and reminding me of my mother's goodness: I had asked her to make some vanilla ice cream for my first day of vacation, and when I woke up I could smell it.

It was half past ten. I lit a cigarette, pushed up my pillow, and considered how I would spend the afternoon. I decided to go swimming; after lunch I would take the streetcar to the beach, have a bit of a swim, read, smoke, and wait for one of the girls at the office who had promised to come down to the beach after five.

In the kitchen my mother was pounding meat, and when she stopped for a moment I could hear her humming a tune. It was a hymn. I felt very happy. The previous day I had passed my test, I had a good job in a textile factory, a job with opportunities for advancement —but now I was on vacation, two weeks' vacation, and it was summertime. It was hot outside, but in those days I still loved hot weather: through the slits in the shutters I could see the heat haze, I could see the green of the trees in front of our house, I could hear the streetcar. And I was looking forward to breakfast. Then I heard my mother coming to listen at my door; she crossed the hall, stopped by my door, it was silent for a moment in our apartment, and I was just about to call "Mother" when the bell rang downstairs. My mother went to our front door, and I heard the funny high-pitched purring of the buzzer down below, it buzzed four, five, six times, my mother was talking on the landing to Frau Kurz, who lived in the next apartment. Then I heard a man's voice, and I knew at once it was the mailman, although I had only seen him a few times. The mailman came into our entrance hall, Mother said: "What?" and he said: "Here—sign here, please." It was very quiet for a moment, the mailman said "Thanks," my mother closed the door after him, and I heard her go back into the kitchen.

Shortly after that I got up and went into the bathroom. I shaved, had a leisurely wash, and when I turned off the faucet I could hear my mother grinding the coffee. It was like Sunday, except that I had not been to church.

Nobody will believe it, but my heart suddenly felt heavy. I don't know why, but it was heavy. I could no longer hear the coffee mill. I dried myself off, put on my shirt and trousers, socks and shoes, combed my hair and went into the living room. There were flowers on the table, pale pink carnations, it all looked fresh and neat, and on my plate lay a red pack of cigarettes.

Then Mother came in from the kitchen carrying the coffeepot and I saw at once she had been crying. In one hand she was holding the coffeepot, in the other a little pile of mail, and her eyes were red. I went over to her, took the pot from her, kissed her cheek and said: "Good morning." She looked at me, said: "Good morning, did you sleep well?" and tried to smile, but did not succeed.

We sat down, my mother poured the coffee, and I opened the red pack lying on my plate and lit a cigarette. I had suddenly lost my appetite. I stirred milk and sugar into my coffee, tried to look at Mother, but each time I quickly lowered my eyes. "Was there any mail?" I asked, a senseless question, since Mother's small red hand was resting on the little pile on top of which lay the newspaper.

"Yes," she said, pushing the pile toward me. I opened the newspaper while my mother began to butter some bread for me. The front page bore the headline: "Outrages continue against Germans in the Polish Corridor!" There had been headlines like that for weeks on the front pages of the papers. Reports "of rifle fire along the Polish border and refugees escaping from the sphere of Polish harassment and fleeing to the Reich." I put the paper aside. Next I read the brochure of a wine merchant who used to supply us sometimes when Father was still alive. Various types of Riesling were being offered at exceptionally low prices. I put the brochure aside too.

Meanwhile my mother had finished buttering the slice of bread for me. She put it on my plate saying: "Please eat something!" She burst into violent sobs. I could not bring myself to look at her. I can't look at anyone who is really suffering—but now for the first time I realized it must have something to do with the mail. It must be the mail. I stubbed out my cigarette, took a bite of the bread-and-butter and picked up the next letter, and as I did so I saw there was a post card lying underneath. But I had not noticed the registration sticker, that tiny scrap of paper I

still possess and to which I owe a reputation for sentimentality. So I read the letter first. The letter was from
Uncle Eddy. Uncle Eddy wrote that at last, after many
years as an assistant instructor, he was now a full-
fledged teacher, but it had meant being transferred to a
little one-horse town; financially speaking, he was hardly
any better off than before, since he was now being
paid at the local scale. And his kids had had whooping
cough, and the way things were going made him feel sick
to his stomach, he didn't have to tell us why. No, he
didn't, and it made us feel sick too. It made a lot of people feel sick.

When I reached for the post card I saw it had gone.
My mother had picked it up, she was holding it up and
looking at it, and I kept my eyes on my half-eaten slice
of bread, stirred my coffee and waited.

I shall never forget it. Only once had my mother ever
cried so terribly: when my father died; and then I had
not dared to look at her either. A nameless diffidence
had prevented me from comforting her.

I tried to bite into the bread, but my throat closed up,
for I suddenly realized that what was upsetting Mother
so much could only be something to do with me. Mother
said something I didn't catch and handed me the post
card, and it was then I saw the registration sticker: that
red-bordered rectangle, divided by a red line into two
other rectangles, of which the smaller one contained a
big black R and the bigger one the word "Düsseldorf"
and the number 634. Otherwise the post card was quite
normal, it was addressed to me and on the back were the

words: "Mr. Bruno Schneider: You are required to report on August 5, 1939, to the Schlieffen Barracks in Adenbrück for an eight-week period of military training." The words Bruno Schneider, the date and Adenbrück were typed, everything else was printed, and at the bottom was a vague scrawl and the printed word "Major."

Today I know that the scrawl was superfluous. A machine for printing majors' signatures would do the job just as well. The only thing that mattered was the little sticker on the front for which my mother had had to sign a receipt.

I put my hand on her arm and said: "Now look, Mother, it's only eight weeks." And my mother said: "I know."

"Only eight weeks," I said, and I knew I was lying, and my mother dried her tears, said: "Yes, of course," we were both lying, without knowing why we were lying, but we were and we knew we were.

I was just picking up my bread-and-butter again when it struck me that today was the fourth and that on the following day at ten o'clock I had to be over two hundred miles away to the east. I felt myself going pale, put down the bread and got up, ignoring my mother. I went to my room. I stood at my desk, opened the drawer, closed it again. I looked round, felt something had happened and didn't know what. The room was no longer mine. That was all. Today I know, but that day I did meaningless things to reassure myself that the room still belonged to me. It was useless to rummage around in the box containing my letters, or to straighten my books. Before I knew what I was doing I had begun to pack my briefcase: shirt, pants, towel and socks, and I went into the bathroom to get my shaving things. My mother was still sitting at the breakfast table. She had stopped crying. My half-eaten slice of bread was still on my plate, there was still some coffee in my cup, and I said to my mother: "I'm going over to the Giesselbachs to phone about my train."

When I came back from the Giesselbachs it was just striking twelve noon. Our entrance hall smelled of roast pork and cauliflower, and my mother had begun to break up ice in a bag to put into our little ice-cream machine.

My train was leaving at eight that evening, and I would be in Adenbrück next morning about six. It was only fifteen minutes' walk to the station, but I left the house at three o'clock. I lied to my mother, who did not know how long it took to get to Adenbrück.

Those last three hours I spent in the house seem, on looking back, worse and longer than the whole time I spent away, and that was a long time. I don't know what we did. We had no appetite for dinner. My mother soon took back the roast, the cauliflower, the potatoes, and the vanilla ice cream to the kitchen. Then we drank the breakfast coffee which had been kept warm under a yellow cosy, and I smoked cigarettes, and now and again we exchanged a few words. "Eight weeks," I said, and my mother said: "Yes—yes, of course," and she didn't cry any more. For three hours we lied to each other, till I couldn't stand it any longer. My mother blessed me, kissed me on both cheeks, and as I closed the front door behind me I knew she was crying.

I walked to the station. The station was bustling with activity. It was vacation time: happy sun-tanned people were milling around. I had a beer in the waiting room and about half past three decided to call up the girl from the office whom I had arranged to meet at the beach.

While I was dialing the number, and the perforated nickel dial kept clicking back into place—five times—I almost regretted it, but I dialed the sixth figure, and when her voice asked: "Who is it?" I was silent for a moment, then said slowly: "Bruno" and: "Can you come? I have to go off—I've been drafted."

"Right now?" she asked.

"Yes."

She thought it over for a moment, and through the phone I could hear the voices of the others, who were apparently collecting money to buy some ice cream.

"All right," she said, "I'll come. Are you at the station?"

"Yes," I said.

She arrived at the station very quickly, and to this day I don't know, although she has been my wife now for ten years, to this day I don't know whether I ought to regret that phone call. After all, she kept my job open for me with the firm, she revived my defunct ambition when I came home, and she is actually the one I have to thank for the fact that those opportunities for advancement have now become reality.

But I didn't stay as long as I could have with her either. We went to the movies, and in the cinema, which was empty, dark and very hot, I kissed her, though I didn't feel much like it.

I kept on kissing her, and I went to the station at six o'clock, although I need not have gone till eight. On the platform I kissed her again and boarded the first eastbound train. Ever since then I have not been able to look at a beach without a pang: the sun, the water, the cheerfulness of the people seem all wrong, and I prefer to stroll alone through the town on a rainy day and go to a movie where I don't have to kiss anybody. My opportunities for advancement with the firm are not yet exhausted. I might become a director, and I probably will, according to the law of paradoxical inertia. For people are convinced I am loyal to the firm and will do a great deal for it. But I am not loyal to it and I haven't the slightest intention of doing anything for it. . . .

Lost in thought I have often contemplated that registration sticker which gave such a sudden twist to my life. And when the tests are held in summer and our young employees come to me afterward with beaming faces to be congratulated, it is my job to make a little speech in which the words "opportunities for advancement" play a traditional role.

Unexpected guests

I have nothing against animals; on the contrary, I like them, and I enjoy caressing our dog's coat in the evening while the cat sits on my lap. It gives me pleasure to watch the children feeding the tortoise in the corner of the living room. I have even grown fond of the baby hippopotamus we keep in our bathtub, and the rabbits running around loose in our apartment have long ceased to worry me. Besides, I am used to coming home in the evening and finding an unexpected visitor: a cheeping baby chick, or a stray dog my wife has taken in. For my wife is a good woman, she never turns anyone away from the door, neither man nor beast, and for many years now our children's evening prayers have wound up with the words: O Lord, please send us beggars and animals.

What is really worse is that my wife cannot say no to hawkers and peddlers, with the result that things accumulate in our home which I regard as superfluous: soap, razor blades, brushes and darning wool, and lying around in drawers are documents which cause me some concern: an assortment of insurance policies and pur-

chase agreements. My sons are insured for their education, my daughters for their trousseaux, but we cannot
feed them with either darning wool or soap until they get
married or graduate, and it is only in exceptional cases
that razor blades are beneficial to the human system.

It will be readily understood, therefore, that now and
again I show signs of slight impatience, although gener-
ally speaking I am known to be a quiet man. I often
catch myself looking enviously at the rabbits who have
made themselves at home under the table, munching
away peacefully at their carrots, and the stupid gaze of
the hippopotamus, who is hastening the accumulation of
silt in our bathtub, causes me at times to stick out my
tongue at him. And the tortoise stoically eating its way
through lettuce leaves has not the slightest notion of the
anxieties that swell my breast: the longing for some
fresh, fragrant coffee, for tobacco, bread and eggs, and
the comforting warmth engendered by a schnapps in the
throats of careworn men. My sole comfort at such times
is Billy, our dog, who, like me, is yawning with hunger.
If, on top of all this, unexpected guests arrive—men unshaven like myself, or mothers with babies who get fed
warm milk and moistened zwieback—I have to get a
grip on myself if I am to keep my temper. But I do keep
it, because by this time it is practically the only thing I
have left.

There are days when the mere sight of freshly boiled,
snowy potatoes makes my mouth water; for—although I
confess this reluctantly and with deep embarrassment—
it is a long time since we have enjoyed "good home

cooking." Our only meals are improvised ones of which we partake from time to time, standing up, surrounded by animals and human guests.

Fortunately it will be a while before my wife can buy useless articles again, for we have no more cash, my wages have been attached for an indefinite period, and I myself am reduced to spending the evenings going around the distant suburbs, in clothing that makes me unrecognizable, selling razor blades, soap and buttons far below cost; for our situation has become grave. Nevertheless, we own several hundredweight of soap, thousands of razor blades, and buttons of every description, and toward midnight I stagger into the house and go through my pockets for money: my children, my animals, my wife stand around me with shining eyes, for I have usually bought some things on the way home: bread, apples, lard, coffee and potatoes—the latter, by the way, in great demand among the children as well as the animals—and during the nocturnal hours we gather together for a cheerful meal: contented animals, contented children are all about me, my wife smiles at me, and we leave the living-room door open so the hippopotamus will not feel left out, his joyful grunts resounding from the bathroom. At that point my wife usually confesses to me that she has an extra guest hidden in the storeroom, who is only brought out when my nerves have been fortified by food: shy, unshaven men, rubbing their hands, take their place at table, women squeeze in between our children on the bench, milk is warmed up for crying babies. In this way I also make the acquaintance of animals that are new to me: seagulls, foxes and pigs, although once it was a small dromedary.

"Isn't it cute?" asked my wife, and I was obliged to say yes, it was, while I anxiously watched the tireless munching of this duffel-colored creature which looked at us out of slate-gray eyes. Fortunately the dromedary only stayed a week, and business was brisk: word had got round of the quality of my merchandise, my reduced prices, and now and again I was even able to sell shoe-laces and brushes, articles otherwise not much in demand. As a result, we experienced a period of false prosperity, and my wife, completely blind to the economic facts, produced a remark which worried me: "Things are looking up!" But I saw our stocks of soap shrinking, the razor blades dwindling, and even the supply of brushes and darning wool was no longer substantial.

Just about this time, when I could have used some spiritual sustenance, our house was shaken one evening, while we were all sitting peacefully together, by a tremor resembling a fair-sized earthquake: the pictures rattled, the table rocked, and a ring of fried sausage rolled off my plate. I was about to jump up and see what the matter was when I noticed suppressed laughter on the faces of my children. "What's going on here?" I shouted, and for the first time in all my checkered experience I was really beside myself.

"Wilfred," said my wife quietly and put down her fork, "it's only Wally." She began to cry, and against her tears I have no defence, for she has borne me seven children.

"Who is Wally?" I asked wearily, and at that moment the house was rocked by another tremor. "Wally," said my youngest daughter, "is the elephant we've got in the basement."

I must admit I was at a loss, which is not really surprising. The largest animal we had housed so far had been the dromedary, and I considered an elephant too big for our apartment.

My wife and children, not in the least at a loss, supplied the facts: the animal had been brought to us for safekeeping by a bankrupt circus owner. Sliding down the chute which we otherwise use for our coal, it had had no trouble entering the basement. "He rolled himself up into a ball," said my oldest son, "really an intelligent animal." I did not doubt it, accepted the fact of Wally's presence, and was led down in triumph into the basement. The animal was not as large as all that; he waggled his ears and seemed quite at home with us, especially as he had a bale of hay at his disposal. "Isn't he cute?" asked my wife, but I refused to agree. Cute did not seem to be the right word. Anyway the family appeared disappointed at the limited extent of my enthusiasm, and my wife said, as we left the basement: "How cruel you are, do you want him to be put up for auction?"

"What d'you mean, auction," I said, "and why cruel? Besides, it's against the law to conceal bankruptcy assets."

"I don't care," said my wife, "nothing must happen to the animal."

In the middle of the night we were awakened by the

circus owner, a diffident, dark-haired man, who asked us whether we had room for one more animal. "It's my sole possession, all I have left in the world. Only for a night. How is the elephant, by the way?"

"He's fine," said my wife, "only I'm a bit worried about his bowels."

"That'll soon settle down," said the circus owner. "It's just the new surroundings. Animals are so sensitive. How about it then: will you take the cat too—just for the night?" He looked at me, and my wife nudged me and said: "Don't be so unkind."

"Unkind," I said, "no, I certainly don't want to be that. If you like, you can put the cat in the kitchen."

"I've got it outside in the car," said the man.

I left my wife to look after the cat and crawled back into bed. My wife was a bit pale when she came to bed, and she seemed to be trembling. "Are you cold?" I asked.

"Yes," she said, "I've got such funny chills."

"You're just tired."

"Maybe," said my wife, but she gave me a queer look as she said it. We slept quietly, but in my dreams I still saw that queer look of my wife's, and a strange compulsion made me wake up earlier than usual. I decided to shave for once.

Lying under our kitchen table was a medium-sized lion; he was sleeping peacefully, only his tail moved gently and made a sound like someone playing with a very light ball.

I carefully lathered my face and tried not to make

any noise, but when I turned my chin to the right to shave my left cheek I saw that the lion had his eyes open and was watching me. "They really do look like cats," I thought. What the lion was thinking I don't know; he went on watching me, and I shaved, without cutting myself, but I must admit it is a strange feeling to shave with a lion looking on. My experience of handling wild beasts was practically non-existent, and I confined myself to looking sternly at the lion, then I dried my face and went back to the bedroom. My wife was already awake, she was just about to say something, but I cut her short and exclaimed: "What's the use of talking about it!" My wife began to cry, and I put my hand on her head and said: "It's unusual, to say the least, you must admit that."

"What isn't unusual?" said my wife, and I had no answer.

Meanwhile the rabbits had awakened, the children were making a racket in the bathroom, the hippopotamus—his name was Gottlieb—was already trumpeting away, Billy was stretching and yawning, only the tortoise was still asleep, but it sleeps most of the time anyway.

I let the rabbits into the kitchen, where their feed box is kept under the cupboard; the rabbits sniffed at the lion, the lion at the rabbits, and my children—uninhibited and used to animals as they are—were already in the kitchen. I almost had the feeling the lion was smiling; my third-youngest son immediately found a name for him: Bombilus. And Bombilus he remained.

The death of Elsa Baskoleit

The basement of the house we used to live in was rented
to a shopkeeper called Baskoleit; there were always
orange crates standing around in the passages, it smelled
of rotten fruit that Baskoleit put out for the garbage
trucks, and from beyond the dim light of the frosted
glass panel we could often hear his voice with its broad
East Prussian dialect complaining about the bad times.
But in his heart of hearts Baskoleit was a cheerful man:
we knew, as surely as only children can know, that his
grumbling was a game, even the way he used to swear at
us, and he would often come up the three or four steps
leading from the basement to the street with his pockets
full of apples and oranges which he tossed to us like
rubber balls.

But the interesting thing about Baskoleit was his
daughter Elsa, of whom we knew that she wanted to be
a dancer. Perhaps she already was one: in any case, she
practiced a great deal, she practiced downstairs in the
basement room with the yellow walls next to Baskoleit's
kitchen: a slender girl with fair hair who stood on the

tips of her toes, dressed in green tights, pale, hovering for minutes like a swan, whirling around, leaping, or doing handsprings. I could watch her from my bedroom window when it got dark; in the yellow rectangle of the windowframe, her thin, green-clad body, her pale strained face and her fair head that sometimes, when she jumped, touched the naked light bulb, which began to swing and for the space of a few seconds expanded the yellow circle of light on the gray courtyard. There were some people who shouted across the courtyard: "Whore!", and I didn't know what a whore was; there were others who shouted: "It's disgusting!", and although I thought I knew what disgusting was, I couldn't believe it had anything to do with Elsa. Then Baskoleit's window would be flung open, and in the steam of the kitchen his big bald head would loom up, and with the light that fell from the open kitchen window into the courtyard he would pour out into the dark courtyard a torrent of oaths of which I didn't understand a single one. At any rate, Elsa's window was soon provided with a curtain, heavy green plush, which let out hardly any light at all, but every evening I would gaze at the faintly glowing rectangle and see her, although I couldn't see her: Elsa Baskoleit in her light green tights, thin and fair-haired, hovering for seconds on end under the naked light bulb.

But before long we moved away, I got older, found out what a whore was, thought I knew what disgusting was, saw dancers, but liked none of them as well as Elsa

Baskoleit, of whom I never heard again. We moved to another town, war came, a long war, and I thought no more of Elsa Baskoleit, I didn't even think of her when we moved back to the old town. I tried my hand at all sorts of jobs, till I became a truckdriver for a wholesale vegetable dealer: handling a truck was the only thing I was good at. Each morning I was given a list, cases of apples and oranges, baskets of plums, and drove into town.

One day, while I was standing on the ramp where my truck was being loaded and checking what the warehouseman was loading on the truck against my list, the bookkeeper emerged from his cubbyhole, which is plastered with banana posters, and asked the warehouseman: "Can we supply Baskoleit?"

"Has he ordered something? Purple grapes?"

"Yes." The bookkeeper removed the pencil from behind his ear and looked at the warehouseman in surprise.

"Once in a while," said the warehouseman, "he orders something: purple grapes, I don't know why; but we can't supply him. Get a move on!" he shouted to the helpers in their gray smocks. The bookkeeper went back to his cubbyhole, and I ceased to check whether they were really loading the stuff that was on my list. I saw the rectangular, brightly lit frame of the basement window, I saw Elsa Baskoleit dancing, thin and pale, dressed in bright green, and that morning I took a different route from the one I was supposed to take.

Of the lampposts we had played beside, only one was still standing, and even this one was minus its head, most of the houses were in ruins, and my truck jolted through deep potholes. There was only one child in the street, which used to swarm with children: a pale, dark-haired boy sitting on a bit of broken wall and drawing lines in the whitish dust. He looked up as I drove by, but then let his head droop again. I stopped in front of Baskoleit's house and got out.

His small windows were dusty, pyramids of packages had collapsed, and the green cardboard was black with dirt. I looked up at the patched housewall, hesitatingly opened the door, and stepped slowly down into the shop: there was an acrid smell of damp soup mix, which was stuck together in lumps in a cardboard box by the door, but then I saw Baskoleit's back, saw his gray hair below his cap, and could sense how he disliked having to fill a bottle with vinegar from a big barrel. He evidently didn't know how to manage the spigot properly, the sour fluid ran over his fingers, and down on the floor a puddle had formed, a rotting, sour-smelling place in the wood, which squeaked under his feet. A thin woman in a rust-brown coat was standing by the counter, watching him with indifference. At last he seemed to have filled the bottle, he put in the cork, and once again I said what I had already said at the door, quietly said: "Good morning," but no one answered. Baskoleit put the bottle on the counter, his face was pale and unshaven, and he looked at the woman now and said: "My daughter has died—Elsa—"

"I know," said the woman hoarsely, "I've known that for five years. I need some scouring powder too."

"My daughter has died," said Baskoleit. He looked at the woman as if it had just happened, looked at her helplessly, but the woman said: "The loose kind—a pound." And Baskoleit pulled out a black barrel from under the counter, poked around in it with a metal scoop, and with his trembling hands conveyed some yellowish lumps into a gray paper bag.

"My daughter has died," he said. The woman said nothing, and I looked around, all I could see was some dusty packages of noodles, the vinegar barrel, which had a dripping tap, and the scouring powder and an enamel sign showing a grinning fair-haired boy eating a brand of chocolate that hasn't existed for years. The woman put the bottle into her shopping-bag, stuffed the scouring powder in next to it, threw a few coins onto the counter, and as she turned round and walked past me she tapped her forehead briefly with her finger and smiled at me.

I thought of a lot of things, thought of the days when I had been so small that my nose was still below the edge of the counter, but now I could look without effort over the glass showcase bearing the name of a biscuit company and now containing only dusty packets of breadcrumbs; for a few seconds I seemed to shrink, I felt my nose below the dirty edge of the counter, felt the pennies for candies in my hand, I saw Elsa Baskoleit dancing, heard people shouting across the courtyard: "Whore!" and "It's disgusting!" till I was roused by Baskoleit's voice.

"My daughter has died." He said it mechanically, almost without emotion, he was standing by the showcase now, looking out into the street.

"Yes," I said.

"She is dead," he said.

"Yes," I said. He turned his back to me, his hands in the pockets of his gray smock, which was stained.

"She loved grapes—the purple kind, but now she's dead." He did not say: "What would you like?" or "May I help you?", he stood near the dripping vinegar barrel beside the showcase, saying: "My daughter has died" or "She is dead," without looking at me.

I seemed to stand there for an eternity, oblivious and forgotten, while around me time trickled away. It was only when another woman came into the shop that I could rouse myself. She was short and plump, and held her shopping-bag against her stomach, and Baskoleit turned to her and said: "My daughter has died," the woman said: "Yes," began suddenly to cry and said: "Some scouring powder, please, a pound of the loose kind," and Baskoleit went behind the counter and poked around in the barrel with the metal scoop. The woman was still crying when I left.

The pale, dark-haired boy who had been sitting on the bit of broken wall was standing on the running-board of my truck, looking closely at the dashboard. He reached in through the open window and raised the right, then the left indicator. The boy jumped when I suddenly stood behind him, but I grabbed him, looked into his pale frightened face, took an apple from one of the cases on my truck, and gave it to the boy. He looked at me in amazement when I let him go, in such amazement that I was startled, and I took another apple, and another, stuffed them into his pocket, shoved them under his jacket, a lot of apples, before I got in and drove off.

A case for Kop

When Lasnov got back from the station, he brought a message that a case had arrived for Kop. Every day Lasnov met the train from Odessa and tried to make deals with the soldiers. During the first year he had paid for socks, saccharine, salt, matches and lighter-flints with butter and oil—and had enjoyed the generous margins that are always involved in bartering; later on the rates had become more established, and there was tough bargaining over this money that kept on decreasing in value as the fortunes of war declined. There was no more butter to trade, and no oil, and for a long time now none of those juicy hunks of bacon for which in the beginning you could get a French double-bed mattress. Trade had become acute, sour and exasperating, ever since the soldiers had begun to despise their own money. They laughed when Lasnov ran along beside the train with his bundles of notes, calling through the open windows in an agitated, singsong voice: "I pay top prices for everything. Top prices for everything."

Only occasionally did a novice turn up who let him-

self be talked out of a coat or an undervest, carried away
by the sight of the banknotes. And the days were now
few and far between when Lasnov had to negotiate so
long over a more valuable article—a pistol, a watch or
a telescope—that he was obliged to bribe the stationmaster to keep the train waiting till Lasnov had finished his
business. In the early days each minute had cost only a
mark, but the greedy stationmaster, a heavy drinker,
had long since raised the cost of one minute to six
marks.

On this particular morning there had been no business
at all. A gendarme paced up and down alongside the
waiting train, compared his wrist watch with the stationmaster's pocket watch, and shouted at the ragged boy
who ran along by the train looking for cigarette ends.
But the soldiers had stopped throwing away cigarette
ends a long time ago, they would carefully scrape off the
black ash and hoard their remnants of tobacco like jew-
els in their tobacco tins; they were no longer generous
with bread either, and when the boy could not find any
bits of tobacco and ran along by the train waving his
arms and chanting most impressively in a howling singsong voice: "Bread, bread, bread, comrades!," all he got
was a kick from the gendarme; when the train pulled out
he pressed himself against the wall, and a paper bag
rolled to his feet. In it were a slice of bread and an apple. The boy grinned as Lasnov passed him on his way to
the waiting room. The waiting room was empty and cold.
Lasnov left the station and stood outside hesitating. He
felt as if the train had yet to arrive; it had all been over

too quickly, correctly, punctually, but he could hear the rusty creak: the signal arm was slipping back into Stop.

Lasnov jumped when someone put a hand on his shoulder, the hand was too light for the stationmaster's; it was the boy's, and he was holding out the apple he had bitten into and mumbling: "It's so sour, the apple—but what'll you give me for this?" From his left pocket he pulled out a red toothbrush and held it out to Lasnov. Lasnov opened his mouth and involuntarily drew his forefinger across his strong teeth, which felt slightly furry; he shut his mouth, took the toothbrush from the boy, and studied it; its red handle was transparent, the bristles were white and firm.

"A nice Christmas present for your wife," said the boy, "she has such lovely white teeth."

"You monkey," Lasnov said softly, "what are you doing looking at my wife's teeth?"

"Or for your kids," said the boy, "you can look through it—like this." He took the toothbrush from Lasnov, held it up to his eyes, looked at Lasnov, the station, the trees, the dilapidated sugar factory, and gave the brush back to him. "You try," he said, "it looks nice." Lasnov took the brush and held it up to his eyes; on the inside of the handle the refractions were broken: the station looked like a long, long barn, the trees like broken-off brooms, the boy's face was distorted into a squat grimace, the apple he was holding up to his face looked like a red sponge. Lasnov handed the toothbrush back to the boy. "Yes," he said, "not bad at all."

"Ten," said the boy.

"Two."

"No," whimpered the boy, "no, it's so pretty." Lasnov turned away.

"Give me five at least."

"All right," said Lasnov, "here's five." He took the toothbrush and gave the boy the money. The boy ran back into the waiting room, and Lasnov saw him carefully and systematically going through the ashes of the stove with a stick, looking for cigarette ends; a gray cloud of dust rose up, and the boy murmured something to himself in his singsong voice which Lasnov was unable to make out.

The stationmaster came up just when Lasnov had decided to roll a cigarette and was checking his tobacco supply in the palm of his hand, separating the dust from the shreds of tobacco. "Well now," said the stationmaster, "that looks like enough for two." He took some, without asking permission, and the two men stood smoking at the station corner, looking out into the street where booths, stalls and dirty tents were being set up; everything was gray, brown or dirt-colored, there wasn't a spot of color even on the children's carrousel.

"Someone," said the stationmaster, "once gave my kids some coloring books; on one page you could see the finished pictures, in color, and on the opposite page the outlines where you had to put in the colors. But I didn't have any paints, or any crayons either, and the kids filled it all in with pencil—I always have to think of that when I look at this market place. I guess they ran out of colors, all they had was pencil—gray, dirty, dark . . ."

"Yes," said Lasnov, "there's no business at all; the only thing to eat is Rukhev's corn cakes, but you know how he makes those."

"Raw corncobs, pressed together, I know," said the stationmaster, "then smeared with dark-colored oil to make you think they've been cooked in oil."

"Well," said Lasnov, "I'll see if I can't do something anyway."

"If you see Kop, tell him a case has arrived for him."

"A case? What's in it?"

"I don't know. It's from Odessa. I'll send the boy over to Kop with my handcart. Will you let him know?"

"Sure," said Lasnov.

As he strolled through the square he kept looking over to the station to see if the boy was coming with the case. And he told everyone that a case had come for Kop from Odessa. The rumor spread quickly through the market, got ahead of Lasnov, and, as he slowly approached Kop's stall, came back to him on the other side of the street.

When he reached the children's carrousel, the owner was just harnessing the horse: the horse's face was thin and dark, ennobled by hunger: it reminded Lasnov of the nun of Novgorod whom he had once seen as a child. Her face had also been thin and dark, ennobled by abstinence; you could look at her in a dark green tent at fairs, and it had cost nothing to go in, people were merely asked, when they left the tent, to make a donation.

The carrousel owner came up to Lasnov, leaned over and whispered: "Have you heard about the case that's supposed to have come for Kop?"

"No," said Lasnov.

"They say it's got toys in it, cars you can wind up."

"No," said Lasnov, "I heard it was toothbrushes."

"No, no," said the carrousel owner, "toys."

Lasnov stroked the horse's nose affectionately, went wearily on, and thought bitterly of the deals he used to be able to make. He had bought and sold so much clothing that he could have outfitted a whole army, and now he had sunk so low that this kid had talked him into buying a toothbrush. He had sold butter and bacon and barrels of oil, and at Christmas time he had always had a stall with candy canes for the kids; the colors of the candy canes had been as piercing as the joys and sufferings of the poor: red like the love which is celebrated in doorways or beside the factory wall while the bittersweet smell of molasses came wafting over the wall; yellow like the flames in a drunk man's brain, or pale green like the pain you felt when you woke up in the morning and looked at the face of your sleeping wife, a child's face, whose sole protection from life was those frail pink lids, fragile little covers which she had to open as soon as the children began to cry. But this year there weren't even any candy canes, and they would spend Christmas sitting at home, sipping thin soup and taking turns to look through the handle of the toothbrush.

Next to the carrousel a woman had put two old chairs side by side and opened a shop on them: she had two mattresses to sell with the words "Magasin du Louvre" still visible on them, a well-thumbed book entitled "Left and Right of the Railway Line—from Gelsenkirchen to Essen," an English magazine dating from 1938, and a little tin which had once contained a typewriter ribbon.

"Some lovely things," said the old woman when Lasnov stopped beside her.

"Very nice," he said, and was about to move on when the woman pounced on him, drew him by the sleeve, and whispered: "A case has come for Kop from Odessa. With things for Christmas."

"Has it?" he said. "What things?"

"Candy, all colored, and rubber animals that squeak. It's going to be such fun."

"Sure," said Lasnov, "it's going to be fun."

When he finally reached Kop's stall, Kop had just begun to unload his stuff and spread it out: pokers, saucepans, stoves, rusty nails which he always found himself and hammered straight. Nearly everyone had gathered around Kop's stall, they stood there speechless with excitement, looking along the street. As Lasnov went up to him, Kop was just unpacking a firescreen with a design of gold flowers and a Chinese woman.

"I've got a message for you," said Lasnov, "a case has arrived for you. The boy who's always hanging around the station is going to bring it over."

Kop looked at him with a sigh and said quietly: "Now I'm getting it from you too."

"What d'you mean, me too," said Lasnov. "I've come straight here from the station to give you the message."

Kop ducked nervously; he was well-dressed and wore an immaculate gray fur cap, he always carried a stick with which he made dents in the ground as he walked along, and as a sole reminder of his better days he kept a cigarette dangling nonchalantly from his lips, a cigarette which was rarely alight because he rarely had money for tobacco. Twenty-seven years ago, when Lasnov came back to the village as a deserter with the news of the revolution, Kop had been an ensign in command of the railway station, and when Lasnov had entered the station at the head of the Soldiers' Council to arrest him, Kop had been prepared to allow a movement of his lips, the angle of his cigarette, to cost him his life; in any case they all looked at the corner of his mouth, and he realized they might shoot him, but he did not remove the cigarette from his lips when Lasnov approached him. However, Lasnov had merely slapped his face, the cigarette had fallen out of his mouth, and without it he looked like a boy who has forgotten his homework. They had left him in peace; first he had been a teacher, then a dealer, but still whenever he saw Lasnov he was afraid Lasnov would knock the cigarette out of his mouth. He raised his head apprehensively, straightened the firescreen, and said: "If you only knew how many people have told me that already."

"A firescreen," said a woman, "if only one had

enough heat to shield oneself from it with a firescreen."
Kop looked at her contemptuously. "You have no sense
of beauty."

"No," said the woman with a laugh, "I'm beautiful
myself, and look at all the nice kids I've got." She ran
her hand lightly over the heads of the four children
grouped around her. "You don't..." She looked up
quickly as her children suddenly ran off toward the station, following the other children, toward the boy who
was bringing Kop's case on the stationmaster's handcart.

Everyone hurried away from their stalls, the children
jumped down off the carrousel.

"My God," whispered Kop to Lasnov, the only one
who had stayed behind, "I could almost wish the case
hadn't come. They'll tear me to pieces."

"Don't you know what's in it?"

"No idea," said Kop, "I only know it must be made of
tin."

"There's a lot of things can be made of tin—cans,
toys, spoons."

"Music-boxes—the kind you turn with a handle."

"Yes—just imagine."

Kop and Lasnov helped the boy lift the case down off
the cart; the case was white, made of fresh, smooth
boards, and it was nearly as high as the table on which
Kop had spread out his rusty nails, pokers and scissors.

Everyone fell silent as Kop thrust an old poker under
the lid of the case and slowly raised it up; you could
hear the faint creak of the nails. Lasnov wondered where
all the people had suddenly sprung from; he was star-

tled when the boy suddenly said: "I know what's inside."

No one asked, they all looked at him in suspense, and the boy looked silently at the tense faces; he broke out in a sweat and said in a low voice: "Nothing—there's nothing inside."

If he had said that one second earlier, they would have fallen on him and beaten him up in their disappointment, but now Kop had just taken the lid off and was groping around in the shavings; he removed a whole layer of shavings, then another, then screwed-up paper —then he held up both hands filled with the things he had found in the center of the case. "Tweezers," a woman cried out, but they weren't.

"No," said the woman who had called herself beautiful, "no, they're . . ."

"What are they?" said a little boy.

"Sugar tongs, that's what they are," said the carrousel owner in a dry voice, then he suddenly let out a wild laugh, threw up his arms, and ran back to his carrousel, still roaring with laughter.

"So they are," said Kop, "they're sugar tongs— dozens of them." He threw the tongs he was holding back into the case and groped around in it, but although they could not see his face they all knew he was not smiling. He ran his hands through the clinking metal tongs the way misers in paintings finger their treasures.

"Isn't that just like them?" said one woman, "sugar tongs . . . I really believe if there was such a thing as sugar I could manage to pick it up in my fingers, eh?"

"I had a grandmother," said Lasnov, "who always

picked sugar up in her fingers—but then she was a dirty peasant woman."

"I think I could bring myself to do that too."

"You always were a pig anyhow, picking sugar up in your fingers. Ugh."

"You could use them," said Lasnov, "to fish tomatoes out of jars."

"Provided you had any tomatoes," said the woman who had called herself beautiful. Lasnov looked at her closely. She really was beautiful; she had plentiful fair hair, a straight nose, and fine dark eyes.

"You could also use them," said Lasnov, "for pickles."

"If you had any," said the woman.

"You could use them to pinch yourself in the behind."

"If you still had one," said the woman coldly. Her expression was becoming more and more angry and beautiful.

"You could pick up coal with them too."

"If you had any."

"You could use them as a cigarette holder."

"If you had anything to smoke."

Whenever Lasnov spoke, they all turned toward him, and as soon as he had finished they all turned toward the woman, and the more ridiculous the sugar tongs became in this dialogue, the more empty and miserable became the faces of the children and their parents. I must make them laugh, thought Lasnov. I was afraid there would be toothbrushes in the case, but sugar tongs are really even worse. He blushed under the woman's triumphant gaze and said loudly: "You could use them to serve boiled fish."

"If you had any," said the woman.

"The children could play with them," said Lasnov in a low voice.

"If you . . . ," began the woman, then she suddenly laughed out loud, and everyone else laughed too, for children were something they all had plenty of.

"All right," said Lasnov to Kop, "I'll take three, how much are they?"

"Twelve," said Kop.

"Twelve," said Lasnov and threw the money down on Kop's table. "It's a real bargain."

"It's really not expensive," said Kop shyly.

Ten minutes later all the children were running about the square with their sugar tongs glittering like silver, they sat on the carrousel, pinched their noses with them, brandished them in front of the grownups.

The boy who had brought the case over had been given one too. He sat on the steps in front of the station and hammered his sugar tongs flat. Now at last, he thought, I've got something I can use to get in between the cracks of the floorboards. Of course he had never thought of this. He had tried with pokers, scissors, and bits of wire, but he had never been able to manage it. He was sure he would be able to now he had this tool.

Kop counted his money, stacked it, and placed it carefully in his wallet. He looked at Lasnov, who was standing beside him, gloomily watching the activity in the square.

"You could do me a favor," said Kop.

"What favor," said Lasnov absent-mindedly, without looking at Kop.

"Slap my face," said Kop, "hard enough for the cigarette to fall out."

Lasnov, still without looking at Kop, shook his head thoughtfully.

"Do that," said Kop, "please do. Don't you remember?"

"I remember," said Lasnov, "but I don't feel like doing it again."

"Are you sure?"

"Yes," said Lasnov, "I'm sure, I've never thought of doing it again."

"Damn it," said Kop, "and here I've been dreading it for twenty-seven years."

"You didn't have to," said Lasnov. He walked back to the station shaking his head. There's still a chance, he thought, that they'll run a special, a leave train or one for the wounded; specials didn't come very often, but just the same there might still be one today. He thoughtfully fingered the toothbrush and the three sugar tongs in his coat pocket. There have been times, he thought, when three special trains have arrived in one day.

He leaned against the lamppost in front of the station and scraped the last of his tobacco into a little heap. . . .

This is Tibten!

Soulless people cannot understand why I take such pains and humble pride in performing duties which they regard as beneath my dignity. My occupation may not correspond to my level of education, nor was it foretold by my fairy godmother at my christening, but I enjoy my work, and it provides me with a living: I tell people where they are. Passengers who in the evening at their own railway stations board trains which carry them to distant places, and who then during the night wake up at our station, peer out, confused, into the darkness, not knowing whether they have gone beyond their destination or have not yet reached it, or are possibly even at their destination (for our town contains a variety of tourist attractions and draws many visitors)—I tell all these people where they are. I switch on the loudspeaker as soon as a train arrives and the wheels of the locomotive have come to a standstill, and I say diffidently into the night: "This is Tibten—you are now in Tibten! Passengers wishing to visit the tomb of Tiburtius must alight here!", and the echo comes back to me from the platforms, right into my cubbyhole: a dark voice out of the darkness which seems to be announcing something doubtful, although actually it is speaking the plain truth.

A number of passengers then hurriedly descend onto the dimly lit platform, carrying their suitcases, for Tibten is their destination, and I watch them go down the stairs, reappear on Platform 1, and hand over their tickets to the sleepy ticket collector at the barrier. Very few people arrive on business at night—businessmen intending to fill their companies' requirements at the Tibten lead mines. The visitors are mostly tourists attracted by the tomb of Tiburtius, a young Roman boy who committed suicide eighteen hundred years ago for the sake of a Tibten beauty. "He was but a lad," is inscribed on his tombstone, which can be admired in our local museum, "yet Love was his undoing!" He came here from Rome to purchase lead for his father, who was an army contractor.

Certainly I would not have had to attend five universities and obtain two doctorates in order to be able to call out night after night into the darkness: "This is Tibten! You are now in Tibten!" And yet my work fills me with satisfaction. I speak my lines softly, so that those who are asleep do not wake up but those who are awake will not fail to hear it, and I make my voice sound just enticing enough for those who are dozing to rouse themselves and wonder whether they had not meant to go to Tibten.

In the latter part of the morning, therefore, when I wake up and look out of the window, I can see the passengers who succumbed to the spell of my voice making their way through our little town, armed with the brochures which our travel bureau so generously distributes all over the world. At breakfast they have already read that the wear and tear of centuries has reduced the Latin Tiburtinum to its present form of Tibten, and they proceed to the local museum, where they admire the tombstone erected eighteen hundred years ago to the Roman Werther. A boy's profile has been chiseled out of reddish sandstone, his hands outstretched in vain toward a girl. "He was but a lad, yet Love was his undoing. . . ." His youthfulness is also attested to by the objects which were found in his grave: little figures made of some ivory-colored substance; two elephants, a horse, and a mastiff, which—as Brusler claims in his "Theory of the Tomb of Tiburtius"—were said to have been used in a kind of chess game. I doubt this theory, however. I am sure that to Tiburtius these objects were simply toys. The little ivory objects look exactly like the ones we get as a premium when we buy half a pound of margarine, and they served the same purpose: they were for children to play with. . . . Possibly it behooves me to refer here to the excellent novel written by our local author, Volker von Volkersen, entitled "Tiburtius, a Roman Destiny Which Found Fulfilment in Our Town." But I regard Volkersen's book as misleading, because he also supports Brusler's theory as to the purpose of the toys.

I myself—at this point I must at last make a confession—am in possession of the original figures contained in Tiburtius' grave; I stole them from the museum and replaced them with the ones I obtain as a

premium with half a pound of margarine: two elephants, a horse, and a mastiff; they are as white as
Tiburtius' animals, they are the same size, the same
weight, and—what seems to me most important of all—
they serve the same purpose.

So tourists come from all over the world to admire the
tomb of Tiburtius and his toys. Posters saying "Come to
Tibten" hang in the waiting rooms of the Anglo-Saxon
world, and when at night I speak my lines: "This is Tibten! You are in Tibten! Passengers wishing to visit the
tomb of Tiburtius must alight here . . . ," I lure out of
the trains the people who at their own railway stations
succumbed to the spell of our posters. To be sure, they
look at the sandstone slab, the authenticity of which is
unquestioned. They look at the touching profile of a
Roman boy for whom Love was his undoing and who
drowned himself in a flooded shaft of the lead mines.
And then the visitors' eyes move to the little animals:
two elephants, a horse, and a mastiff—and this is just
where they could study the wisdom of the world, but
they do not. Ladies from our own and other countries,
deeply moved, pile roses onto the tomb of this young
lad. Poems are written; even my animals, the horse and
the mastiff (I had to use up two pounds of margarine to
acquire them!) have already become the subject of lyri-
cal endeavors. "Thou didst play, even as we play, with
mastiff and horse . . ." goes one line in the verses written
by a not unknown poet. So there they lie: free gifts from
the "Klüsshenn Margarine Company," on red velvet under heavy glass in our local museum: witnesses to my

consumption of margarine. Often, before I go on shift in the afternoon, I visit the museum for a minute and study them: they look genuine, slightly yellowed, and are completely indistinguishable from the ones lying in my drawer, for I threw in the originals among those I got with Klüsshenn's margarine, and I try in vain to separate them again.

Deep in thought I then go off to work, hang up my cap on the hook, take off my coat, place my sandwiches in the drawer, arrange my cigarette papers, tobacco and newspaper, and, when a train arrives, speak the lines which it is my job to speak: "This is Tibten! You are now in Tibten! Passengers wishing to visit the tomb of Tiburtius must alight here. . . ." I speak them softly, so that those who are asleep do not wake up, and those who are awake will not fail to hear me, and I make my voice sound just enticing enough for those who are dozing to rouse themselves and wonder whether they had not meant to go to Tibten.

And I cannot understand why anyone regards this work as beneath my dignity. . . .

And there was the evening and the morning....

It was not until noon that he thought of leaving his Christmas presents for Anna in the baggage room at the station; he was glad he had thought of it, for it meant he didn't have to go home immediately. Ever since Anna had stopped speaking to him he was afraid of going home; her silence bore down on him like a tombstone the minute he entered the apartment. He used to look forward to going home, for two years after his wedding-day: he loved having supper with Anna, talking to her, and then going to bed; best of all he loved the hour between going to bed and falling asleep. Anna fell asleep earlier than he did because nowadays she was always tired—and he would lie there in the darkness beside her, he could hear her breathing, and from the far end of the street the headlamps of cars now and again threw rays of light onto the ceiling, light that curved down as the cars reached the rise in the street, bands of pale yellow light that made his sleeping wife's profile leap up for a second against the wall; then darkness would fall once more over the room, and all that remained was delicate whorls: the pattern of the curtains drawn on the ceiling by the gaslamp in the street. This was the hour he loved more than any hour of the day, because he could feel the day falling away from him, and he would slide down into sleep as into a bath.

Now he strolled hesitatingly past the baggage counter, and saw his box still there at the back between the red suitcase and the demijohn. The open elevator coming down from the platform was empty, white with snow: it descended like a piece of paper into the gray concrete of the baggage room, and the man who had been operating it walked over and said to the clerk: "Now it really feels like Christmas. It's nice when there's snow for the kids, eh?" The clerk nodded, silently impaled baggage checks on his spike, counted the money in his drawer and looked suspiciously across to Brenig, who had taken his claim check out of his pocket but folded it up and put it back again. This was the third time he had come, the third time he had taken the claim check out and put it back in his pocket again. The clerk's suspicious glances made him uncomfortable; he strolled over to the exit and stood looking out onto the empty station square. He loved the snow, loved the cold; as a boy it had intoxicated him to breathe in the cold clear air, and now he threw away his cigarette and held his face against the wind, which was driving light, profuse snowflakes toward the station. Brenig kept his eyes open, for he liked it when the flakes got caught in his eyelashes, new ones constantly replacing the old which melted and ran down his cheeks in little drops. A girl walked quickly past him, and he saw how her green hat became white with snow while she hurried across the square, but it was only when she was standing at the streetcar stop that he recognized the little red suitcase she was carrying as the one which had stood next to his box in the baggage room.

It was a mistake to get married, thought Brenig; they congratulate you, send you flowers, have stupid telegrams delivered to your door, and then they leave you alone. They ask whether you have thought of everything: of things for the kitchen, from salt-shaker to stove, and finally they make sure you even have plenty of soup-seasoning on the shelf. They estimate whether you can support a family, but what it means to *be* a family is something nobody tells you. They send flowers, twenty bouquets, and it smells like a funeral; then they throw rice and leave you alone.

A man walked past him, and he could tell the man was drunk, he was singing: "Oh come all ye faithful," but Brenig did not shift the angle of his head so that it was a moment or two before he noticed that the man was carrying a demijohn in his right hand, and he knew the box with his Christmas presents for his wife was now standing all by itself on the top shelf of the baggage room. It contained an umbrella, two books, and a big piano made of mocha chocolate: the white keys were of marzipan, the black ones of dark brittle. The chocolate piano was as big as an encyclopedia, and the girl in the store had said the chocolate would keep for six months.

Maybe I was too young to get married, he thought, maybe I should have waited until Anna became less serious and I became more serious, but actually he knew he was serious enough and that Anna's seriousness was just right. That was what he loved about her. For the sake of the hour before falling asleep he had given up movies and dancing, and hadn't even bothered to meet his friends. At night, when he was lying in bed, he was filled with devoutness, with peace, and he would often repeat the sentence to himself, although he wasn't quite certain of the exact wording: "And God made the earth and the moon, to rule over the day and over the night, to divide the light from the darkness, and God saw that it was good, and there was the evening and the morning." He had meant to look it up in Anna's Bible again to see just how it went, but he always forgot. For God to have created day and night seemed to him every bit as wonderful as the creation of flowers, beasts and man.

He loved this hour before falling asleep more than anything else. But now that Anna had stopped speaking to him her silence lay on him like a weight. If she had only said: "It's colder today . . ." or "It's going to rain . . ." it would have put an end to his misery—if she had only said "Yes," or "No, no," or something sillier still, he would be happy, and he would no longer dread going home. But for the space of a few seconds her face would turn to stone, and at these moments he suddenly knew what she would look like as an old woman; he was seized with fear, suddenly saw himself thrust thirty years forward into the future as onto a stony plain, saw himself old too, with the kind of face he had seen on some men: deeply lined with bitterness, strained with suppressed suffering, and tinged to the very nostrils with the light yellow of gall: masks, scattered throughout the everyday world like death's-heads. . . .

Sometimes, although he had only known her for three years, he also knew what she had looked like as a child, he could picture her as a ten-year-old girl, dreaming over a book under the lamplight, grave, her eyes dark under her light lashes, her eyelids flickering above the printed page, her lips parted. . . . Often, when he was sitting opposite her at table, her face would change like the pictures which change when you shake them, and he suddenly knew that she had sat there exactly like that as a child, carefully breaking up her potatoes with her fork and slowly dribbling the gravy over them. . . . The snow had almost stuck his eyelashes together, but he could just make out the Number 4 gliding up over the snow as if on sleds.

Maybe I should phone her, he thought, have her come to the phone at Menders; she'd have to speak to me then. The Number 4 would be followed immediately by the 7, the last streetcar that evening, but by this time he was bitterly cold and he walked slowly across the square, saw the brightly lit blue 7 in the distance, stood undecided by the callbox, and looked in a store window where the window dressers were exchanging Santa Clauses and angels for other dummies: ladies in décolleté, their bare shoulders sprinkled with confetti, their wrists festooned with paper streamers. Their escorts, male dummies with graying temples, were being hurriedly placed on barstools, champagne corks scattered on the floor, one dummy was having its wings and curls taken off, and Brenig was surprised how quickly an angel could be turned into a bartender. Mustache, dark wig and a sign swiftly nailed to the wall saying: "New Year's Eve without champagne?"

Here Christmas was over before it had begun. Maybe, he thought, Anna is too young, she was only twenty-one, and while he contemplated his reflection in the store window he noticed the snow had covered his hair like a little crown—the way he used to see it on fenceposts— and it struck him that old people were wrong to talk about the gaiety of youth: when you were young, everything was serious and difficult, and nobody helped you, and he was suddenly surprised that he did not hate Anna for her silence, that he didn't wish he had married someone else. The whole vocabulary that people offered you was meaningless: forgiveness, divorce, a fresh start, time the Great Healer—these words were all useless. You had to work it out for yourself, because you were different from other people, and because Anna was different from other people's wives.

The window dressers were deftly nailing masks onto the walls, stringing crackers on a cord: the last Number 7 had left long ago, and the box with his presents for Anna was standing all by itself up there on the shelf.

I am twenty-five, he thought, and because of a lie, one little lie, a stupid lie such as millions of men tell every week or every month, I have to endure this punishment; with my eyes staring into the stony future I have to look at Anna crouching like a sphinx on the edge of the stony desert, and at myself, my face yellowed with bitterness, an old man. Oh yes, there would always be plenty of soup-seasoning on the kitchen shelf, the salt-shaker would always be in its proper place, and he would have been a department head for years and well able to support his family: a stony clan, and never again would he lie in bed and in the hour before falling asleep rejoice in the creation of evening, and offer thanks to God for having created rest from the labors of the day, and he would send the same stupid telegrams to young people when they got married as he had been sent himself. . . .

Other women would have laughed over such a stupid lie about his salary, other women knew that all men lie to their wives: maybe it was a kind of instinctive self-defense, against which they invented their own lies, but Anna's face had turned to stone. There were books about marriage, and he had looked up in these books what you could do when something went wrong with your marriage, but none of the books said anything about a woman who had turned to stone. The books told you how to have children and how not to have children, and they contained a lot of big fine words, but the little words were missing.

The window dressers had finished their work: streamers were hanging over wires that were fastened out of sight, and he saw one of the men disappearing at the back of the store with two angels under his arm, while the second man emptied a bag of confetti over the dummy's bare shoulders and gave a final pat to the sign saying "New Year's Eve without champagne?"

Brenig brushed the snow from his hair, walked back across the square to the station, and when he had taken the claim check from his pocket and smoothed it out for the fourth time he ran quickly as if he hadn't a second to lose. But the baggage room was closed, and there was a sign hanging in front of the grille: "Will be opened ten minutes before arrival or departure of a train." Brenig laughed, he laughed for the first time since noon and looked at his box, lying up there on the shelf behind bars as if it was in prison. The departure board was right next to the counter, and he saw the next train would not be arriving for another hour. I can't wait that long, he thought, and at this time of night I won't even be able to get flowers or chocolate, not even a little book, and the last Number 7 has gone. For the first time in his life he thought of taking a taxi, and he felt very grown-up, and at the same time a bit foolish, as he ran across the square to the taxi rank.

He sat in the back of the cab, clasping his money: ten marks, the last of his cash, which he had set aside to buy something special for Anna, but he hadn't found anything special, and now he was sitting there clasping his money and watching the meter jump up at short intervals —very short intervals, it seemed to him—ten pfennigs at a time, and every time the meter clicked it felt like a stab in the heart, although it only showed two marks eighty. Here I am coming home, with no flowers, no presents, hungry, tired and stupid, and it occurred to him that he could almost certainly have got some chocolate in the waiting room at the station.

The streets were empty, the cab drove almost soundlessly through the snow, and in the lighted windows Brenig could see the Christmas trees glowing in the houses: Christmas, the way he had known it as a child and the way he had felt today, seemed very far away: the important things, the things that mattered, happened independently of the calendar, and in the stony desert Christmas would be like any other day of the year and Easter like a rainy day in November: thirty, forty torn-off calendars, metal holders with shreds of paper, that's all that would be left if you didn't watch out.

He was roused by the driver saying: "Here we are. . . ." Then he was relieved to see that the meter had stopped at three marks forty. He waited impatiently for his change from five marks, and he felt a surge of relief when he saw a light upstairs in the room where Anna's bed stood next to his. He made up his mind never to forget this moment of relief, and as he got out his house key and put it in the door, he experienced that silly feeling again that he had had when he got into the taxi: he felt grown-up, yet at the same time a bit foolish.

In the kitchen the Christmas tree was standing on the table, with presents spread out for him: socks, cigarettes and a new fountain pen, and a gay, colorful calendar which he would be able to hang over his desk in the office. The milk was already in the saucepan on the stove, he had only to light the gas, and there were sandwiches ready for him on the plate—but that was how it had been every evening, even since Anna had stopped speaking to him, and the setting up of the Christmas tree and the laying out of the presents was like the preparing of the sandwiches—a duty, and Anna would always do her duty. He didn't feel like the milk, and the appetizing sandwiches didn't appeal to him either. He went into the little hall and noticed at once that Anna had turned out the light. But the door to the bedroom was open, and without much hope he called softly into the dark rectangle: "Anna, are you asleep?" He waited, for a long time it seemed, as if his question was falling into a deep well, and the dark silence in the dark rectangle of the bedroom door contained everything that was in store for him in thirty, forty years—and when Anna said "No," he thought he must have heard wrong, perhaps it was an illusion, and he went on hurriedly in a louder voice: "I've done such a stupid thing. I checked my presents for you at the station, and when I wanted to pick them up the baggage room was closed, and I didn't want to hang around. Are you angry?"

This time he was sure he had really heard her "No," but he could also hear that this "No" did not come from the corner of the room where their beds had been. Evidently Anna had moved her bed under the window. "It's an umbrella," he said, "two books and a little piano made of chocolate; it's as big as an encyclopedia, the keys are made of marzipan and brittle." He stopped, listened for a reply, nothing came from the dark rectangle, but when he asked: "Are you pleased?" the "Yes" came quicker than the two "No's" had done. . . .

The adventure

Fink walked over to the side entrance of the church. Right and left of the cracked asphalt were tiny triangular garden plots bordered with black iron railings: sour, gray-black earth and two box shrubs with leaves as tough and desiccated as leather. Leaning his shoulder against the brown padded door, he opened it and found himself in a musty entrance with another padded door ahead. This one he punched open with his fist, and before entering the church he glanced at a notice on a plywood board which read: "Third Order of St. Francis— Announcements. . . ."

The church was filled with a greenish half-light, and on a wall painted a nondescript color Fink saw a white placard showing a hand, done in black, pointing straight down. Above the stiff, exaggeratedly long forefinger were the words: Confessional Bell. Underneath, in brown holders, were bell-pushes of dark ivory, and name plates. He did not bother to decipher the names but pressed one of the buttons at random, and it seemed to him that this act represented something irrevocable, final. Then he listened—not a sound.

He dipped his finger into a pink plaster stoup in the form of a shell; in the dim light it resembled a great artificial palate with a few bits chipped out of it. Slowly he crossed himself and entered the center nave. On either side he saw two dark confessionals, their red curtains drawn shut, and he now noticed that bomb damage had caused the stucco roof between the gothic columns to crumble away: the ugly masonry of yellow brick was laid bare, somehow it reminded him of an old-fashioned public bathhouse. What was once the main entrance had been walled up with rough stones, and squashed in among them was a crooked old window frame from which the white paint had flaked off.

Fink knelt down in the center nave and tried to pray, but over his folded hands he had to keep watching the four confessionals and peering into the dimness so as not to miss the priest who might suddenly appear from somewhere. He would probably come from the sacristy, up front, where in the semi-darkness Fink could make out a brass bell with a red velvet rope next to the perpetual light. Toward the middle the church got lighter, and he now saw that the whole center nave had been repaired: the ruined, jagged walls supported temporary, almost flat rafters boarded up with grimy old planks—some of the planks were dark with floor varnish—and the saints against the columns were all minus their heads, a helpless, pathetic double rank of strange plaster figures with their heads knocked off and their emblems torn from their grasp, somber truncated torsos which seemed to be holding out their mutilated hands to him in supplication.

Fink tried to summon feelings of remorse and contrition, but without success; he found it hard to concentrate, and from within him there arose a welter of stumbling, spasmodic, imploring prayers, interspersed with memories and the ever-recurring desire to get all this over with quickly and leave, get out and away from this town.

He could already sense it: the thing he wanted to confess was starting to become a memory, to acquire luster; imperceptibly it was emerging from the level of the sordid daily grind, and it seemed to him that one day, soon —he would somehow rise above it and look down: a beautiful, sinful adventure, while in reality—and this he knew too—he had simply followed the rules of the game out of a sort of politeness, rules so depressingly casual and so grimly serious that he had been appalled. Even before it happened, he had been seized with disgust, but he had joined in the game, persuading himself that after all it was nothing but a mechanical act, dictated by nature, while in his heart he knew that the arrow, already quivering in the bow, was going to be released, and would strike him unerringly in that invisible something for which he could find no other name than soul.

He sighed, and began to feel impatient; in his mind's eye the images—those which were gradually acquiring a golden patina, and the real ones—were hovering beside, above, below one another, occasionally merging for an instant, and his gaze traveled in agonizing suspense past the headless saints against their columns to that velvet rope beside the bell.

It occurred to him that possibly the bell was not even working, or that the priest whose name he had not bothered to read was not there. He was not familiar with this form of confession; in the old days they used to make jokes about it. He was just about to get up and go over to the bell-pushes again when he saw in the motionless background of the empty church a dark figure which emerged from the sacristy, genuflected before the altar, and crossed over to the confessionals on the right-hand side. His tense gaze followed the monk; he was tall and slight, and the circle of hair left by the tonsure was thick and black.

Fink quickly tried once more to summon a sense of remorse and contrition, he silently intoned the formulas he had known by heart for twenty years, and stood up. As he stepped into the aisle he stumbled; somewhere in the red and white tiles with their pattern of lilies there must be a damaged place; he steadied himself against a prayer stool and heard the priest switch off the tiny light and pull the curtain aside. As he knelt down in the airless, dark and very uncomfortable little space and made out the pale ear behind the grille, he felt his heart pounding in his throat; he was too agitated to speak.

"Praise be to Jesus Christ," said a colorless, detached voice.

He forced out a "For ever and ever Amen" and was silent. The sweat was pouring down his back, making his shirt cling to his skin, closely and relentlessly, as if it had been soaked in water; there seemed to be no room left to breathe. The priest cleared his throat.

"I have committed adultery," stammered Fink, and he knew that with that he had said about all he was capable of saying.

"Are you married?"

"No."

"But the woman is?"

"Yes."

"How many times?" The question brought him instantly to his senses. Everything that had been swimming in front of his vision, this large white ear, which looked enormous to him, and the grille—of a strange, crisp brown like the latticework on an apple pie—all this he now saw quite clearly, in all its reality, and he looked into the drooping sleeve of the priest's propped-up arm, a dark cavity between the monk's habit and the pale skin covered with light hairs.

"Once," and a deep involuntary sigh escaped him.

"When?" The questions came tersely, rapidly, impersonally, like a doctor's during an examination.

"Today," he said. Actually it had already receded far into the past for him, but the word brought it back again before his eyes, like a camera zooming toward its object to fix it for ever. One was compelled to look closely at something one did not want to look at closely.

"Avoid seeing this woman."

Now for the first time Fink realized he would be seeing her again; a pretty little housewife with a firm neck and wearing a red housecoat, with eyes which were both boring and sad, and he pictured her with such intensity that he almost missed the priest's question.

"Do you love her?"

He could not say no; to say yes seemed even more monstrous. He thought about it, while the sweat accumulated hot and burning above his eyebrows. "No," he said quickly, adding: "It will be very difficult to avoid seeing her."

The priest was silent, and for a moment Fink saw the lowered lids jerk up, a pair of very quiet gray eyes.

"I am a salesman for a firm that makes prefabricated houses," he said, "and the—the lady has ordered a house from us."

"And you have that territory?"

"Yes." He thought of how he would have to negotiate with her, present plans, discuss estimates, advise on details—countless details which, if one wanted to, could be dragged out for months.

"You must see that you are transferred."

Fink was silent.

The voice became more forceful. "You must do all you can not to see her again. Habit is strong, very strong. You have the sincere desire and resolve not to see the woman again?"

"Yes," said Fink at once, and he knew that for the first time he was really speaking the truth.

"Try; do everything in your power. Think of the Bible message: If thy left hand offend thee, cut it off. Accept the possibility of material loss." He was silent for a moment. "I know it is not easy, but Hell doesn't make things easy for us."

His voice had lost its personal quality again when he said: "Anything else?"

Fink was startled. He was not familiar with this kind of confession, although by this time he realized it was serious, extremely serious, more serious than that regular mechanical hygiene he underwent at home every three months with the chaplain.

"Anything else?" asked the voice impatiently. "When did you last confess?"

"Eight weeks ago."

"And go to Mass?"

"Four."

In a monotonous voice the priest began to intone the Commandments, the way he did with the penitents he was accustomed to, people who scarcely knew the Creed, whose religious vocabulary consisted of Our Father and Hail Mary. Fink was feeling uncomfortable, he wanted to leave.

"No," he said each time quietly, as far as the fifth Commandment. The priest left out the sixth.

"Stealing," said the priest without emotion, "and lying, the seventh and eighth Commandments."

Fink felt his color rising, it surged hot into his ears. For God's sake, he wasn't a thief.

"Have you told a lie?"

Fink said nothing. Never before had anyone asked him whether he had told a lie. In any case it seemed to him he had never confessed before. These crude formulas struck him like hammer blows, and while he was thinking he had never confessed before, he muttered: "Oh well, the houses, our houses are not quite the way they look in the catalogue—I mean, they—people are often disappointed when they actually see them...."

The priest could not suppress an "Aha." He said: "We must be honest about that too, although..." he groped for words, "although it seems impossible. But it is a lie to sell something of whose value one is not convinced." He cleared his throat again, and Fink saw the propped-up arm disappear as the priest began to whisper: "Now we will take it all together and fervently beseech Our Lord Jesus Christ to obtain our forgiveness. He died on the Cross to free us from our sins, and each one of our sins nails Him once more to the Cross. Summon remorse and contrition within yourself again, and as a penance recite one decade of the Sorrowful Mystery."

The priest sat up straight in the center of the confessional, murmuring with closed eyes, then he suddenly turned his face toward Fink again, pronounced the *Absolvo te* in a clear voice, and made the sign of the Cross over him.

"Praise be to Jesus Christ—"

"For ever and ever Amen!" said Fink.

He was stiff all over, and he felt as if hours had gone by. He sat down in a pew and pulled out his handkerchief, and as he began to dry the sweat off he noticed the priest disappearing again into the sacristy.

Fink was tired. He tried to pray, but the words tumbled back inside him like a heavy fall of rock, and while he fought against sleep he saw through half-closed lids that in the dark corner next to the side door candles were now burning in front of the altar of the Mother of God: the cheap paraffin tapers flickered restlessly, consuming themselves in feverish haste, and their shimmer swung the silhouette of a small, old woman onto the wall of the center nave, in gigantic and outlandish detail: single hairs protruding from her forehead stood out hard and black on the wall, a childlike nose and the tired slackness of her lips moving silently: a fleeting memorial, towering above the truncated plaster figures and seeming to grow out beyond the edge of the roof.

Murke's collected silences

Every morning, after entering Broadcasting House, Murke performed an existential exercise. Here in this building the elevator was the kind known as a paternoster—open cages carried on a conveyor belt, like beads on a rosary, moving slowly and continuously from bottom to top, across the top of the elevator shaft, down to the bottom again, so that passengers could step on and off at any floor. Murke would jump onto the paternoster but, instead of getting off at the second floor, where his office was, he would let himself be carried on up, past the third, fourth, fifth floors, and he was seized with panic every time the cage rose above the level of the fifth floor and ground its way up into the empty space where oily chains, greasy rods and groaning machinery pulled and pushed the elevator from an upward into a downward direction, and Murke would stare in terror at the bare brick walls, and sigh with relief as the elevator passed through the lock, dropped into place, and began its slow descent, past the fifth, fourth, third floors. Murke knew his fears were unfounded: obviously nothing would ever happen, nothing could ever happen, and even if it did it could be nothing worse than finding himself up there at the top when the elevator stopped moving and being shut in for an hour or two at the most. He was never without a book in his pocket, and cigarettes; yet as long as the building had been standing, for three years, the elevator had never once failed. On certain days it was inspected, days when Murke had to forego those four and a half seconds of panic, and on these days he was irritable and restless, like people who had gone without breakfast. He needed this panic, the way other people need their coffee, their oatmeal or their fruit juice.

So when he stepped off the elevator at the second floor, the home of the Cultural Department, he felt light-hearted and relaxed, as light-hearted and relaxed as anyone who loves and understands his work. He would unlock the door to his office, walk slowly over to his arm-chair, sit down and light a cigarette. He was always first on the job. He was young, intelligent, and had a pleasant manner, and even his arrogance, which occasionally flashed out for a moment—even that was forgiven him since it was known he had majored in psychology and graduated *cum laude*.

For two days now, Murke had been obliged to go without his panic-breakfast: unusual circumstances had required him to get to Broadcasting House at eight a.m., dash off to a studio and begin work right away, for he had been told by the Director of Broadcasting to go over the two talks on The Nature of Art which the great Bur-

Malottke had taped and to cut them according to Bur-Malottke's instructions. Bur-Malottke, who had converted to Catholicism during the religious fervor of 1945, had suddenly, "overnight," as he put it, "felt religious qualms," he had "suddenly felt he might be blamed for contributing to the religious overtones in radio," and he had decided to omit God, Who occurred frequently in both his half-hour talks on The Nature of Art, and replaced Him with a formula more in keeping with the mental outlook which he had professed before 1945. Bur-Malottke had suggested to the producer that the word God be replaced by the formula "that higher Being Whom we revere," but he had refused to retape the talks, requesting instead that God be cut out of the tapes and replaced by "that higher Being Whom we revere." Bur-Malottke was a friend of the Director, but this friendship was not the reason for the Director's willingness to oblige him: Bur-Malottke was a man one simply did not contradict. He was the author of numerous books of a belletristic-philosophical-religious and art-historical nature, he was on the editorial staff of three periodicals and two newspapers, and closely connected with the largest publishing house. He had agreed to come to Broadcasting House for fifteen minutes on Wednesday and tape the words "that higher Being Whom we revere" as often as God was mentioned in his talks: the rest was up to the technical experts.

It had not been easy for the Director to find someone whom he could ask to do the job; he thought of Murke, but the suddenness with which he thought of Murke made him suspicious—he was a dynamic, robust individual—so he spent five minutes going over the problem in his mind, considered Schwendling, Humkoke, Miss Broldin, but he ended up with Murke. The Director did not like Murke; he had, of course, taken him on as soon as his name had been put forward, the way a zoo director, whose real love is the rabbits and the deer, naturally accepts wild animals too for the simple reason that a zoo must contain wild animals—but what the Director really loved was rabbits and deer, and for him Murke was an intellectual wild animal. In the end his dynamic personality triumphed, and he instructed Murke to cut Bur-Malottke's talks. The talks were to be given on Thursday and Friday, and Bur-Malottke's misgivings had come to him on Sunday night—one might just as well commit suicide as contradict Bur-Malottke, and the Director was much too dynamic to think of suicide.

So Murke spent Monday afternoon and Tuesday morning listening three times to the two half-hour talks on The Nature of Art; he had cut out God, and in the short breaks which he took, during which he silently smoked a cigarette with the technician, reflected on the dynamic personality of the Director and the inferior Being Whom Bur-Malottke revered. He had never read a line of Bur-Malottke, never heard one of his talks before. Monday night he had dreamed of a staircase as tall and steep as the Eiffel Tower, and he had climbed it but soon noticed that the stairs were slippery with soap, and the Director

stood down below and called out: "Go on, Murke, go on
. . . show us what you can do—go on!" Tuesday night
the dream had been similar: he had been at a fair-
ground, strolled casually over to the roller coaster, paid
his thirty pfennigs to a man whose face seemed familiar,
and as he got on the roller coaster he saw that it was at
least ten miles long, he knew there was no going back,
and realized that the man who had taken his thirty
pfennigs had been the Director. Both mornings after
these dreams he had not needed the harmless panic-
breakfast up there in the empty space above the paternoster.

Now it was Wednesday. He was smiling as he entered
the building, got into the paternoster, let himself be carried up as far as the sixth floor—four and a half seconds
of panic, the grinding of the chains, the bare brick walls
—he rode down as far as the fourth floor, got out and
walked toward the studio where he had an appointment
with Bur-Malottke. It was two minutes to ten as he sat
down in his green chair, waved to the technician and lit
his cigarette. His breathing was quiet, he took a piece of
paper out of his breast pocket and glanced at the clock:
Bur-Malottke was always on time, at least he had a reputation for being punctual; and as the second hand completed the sixtieth minute of the tenth hour, the minute
hand slipped onto the twelve, the hour hand onto the ten,
the door opened, and in walked Bur-Malottke. Murke got
up, and with a pleasant smile walked over to Bur-
Malottke and introduced himself. Bur-Malottke shook

hands, smiled and said: "Well, let's get started!" Murke picked up the sheet of paper from the table, put his cigarette between his lips, and, reading from the list, said to Bur-Malottke:

"In the two talks, God occurs precisely twenty-seven times—so I must ask you to repeat twenty-seven times the words we are to splice. We would appreciate it if we might ask you to repeat them thirty-five times, so as to have a certain reserve when it comes to splicing."

"Granted," said Bur-Malottke with a smile, and sat down.

"There is one difficulty, however," said Murke: "where God occurs in the genitive, such as 'God's will,' 'God's love,' 'God's purpose,' He must be replaced by the noun in question followed by the words 'of that higher Being Whom we revere.' I must ask you, therefore, to repeat the words 'the will' twice, 'the love' twice, and 'the purpose' three times, followed each time by 'of that higher Being Whom we revere,' giving us a total of seven genitives. Then there is one spot where you use the vocative and say 'O God'—here I suggest you substitute 'O Thou higher Being Whom we revere.' Everywhere else only the nominative case applies."

It was clear that Bur-Malottke had not thought of these complications; he began to sweat, the grammatical transposition bothered him. Murke went on: "In all," he said, in his pleasant, friendly manner, "the twenty-seven sentences will require one minute and twenty seconds radio time, whereas the twenty-seven times 'God' occurs require only twenty seconds. In other words, in order to take care of your alterations we shall have to cut half a minute from each talk."

Bur-Malottke sweated more heavily than ever; inwardly he cursed his sudden misgivings and asked: "I suppose you've already done the cutting, have you?"

"Yes, I have," said Murke, pulling a flat metal box out of his pocket; he opened it and held it out to Bur-Malottke: it contained some darkish sound-tape scraps, and Murke said softly: "God twenty-seven times, spoken by you. Would you care to have them?"

"No I would not," said Bur-Malottke, furious. "I'll speak to the Director about the two half-minutes. What comes after my talks in the program?"

"Tomorrow," said Murke, "your talk is followed by the regular program Neighborly News, edited by Grehm."

"Damn," said Bur-Malottke, "it's no use asking Grehm for a favor."

"And the day after tomorrow," said Murke, "your talk is followed by Let's Go Dancing."

"Oh God, that's Huglieme," groaned Bur-Malottke, "never yet has Light Entertainment given way to Culture by as much as a fifth of a minute."

"No," said Murke, "it never has, at least—" and his youthful face took on an expression of irreproachable modesty—"at least not since I've been working here."

"Very well," said Bur-Malottke and glanced at the clock, "we'll be through here in ten minutes, I take it, and then I'll have a word with the Director about that minute. Let's go. Can you leave me your list?"

"Of course," said Murke, "I know the figures by heart."

The technician put down his newspaper as Murke entered the little glass booth. The technician was smiling. On Monday and Tuesday, during the six hours they listened to Bur-Malottke's talks and did their cutting, Murke and the technician had not exchanged a single personal word; now and again they exchanged glances, and when they stopped for a breather the technician had passed his cigarettes to Murke and the next day Murke passed his to the technician, and now when Murke saw the technician smiling he thought: If there is such a thing as friendship in this world, then this man is my friend. He laid the metal box with the snippets from Bur-Malottke's talk on the table and said quietly: "Here we go." He plugged into the studio and said into the microphone: "I'm sure we can dispense with the run-through, Professor. We might as well start right away—would you please begin with the nominatives?"

Bur-Malottke nodded, Murke switched off his own microphone, pressed the button which turned on the green light in the studio and heard Bur-Malottke's solemn, carefully articulated voice intoning: "That higher Being Whom we revere—that higher Being . . ."

Bur-Malottke pursed his lips toward the muzzle of the mike as if he wanted to kiss it, sweat ran down his face, and through the glass Murke observed with cold detachment the agony that Bur-Malottke was going through; then he suddenly switched Bur-Malottke off, stopped the moving tape that was recording Bur-Malottke's words, and feasted his eyes on the spectacle of Bur-Malottke behind the glass, soundless, like a fat, handsome fish. He switched on his microphone and his voice came quietly into the studio: "I'm sorry, but our tape was defective, and I must ask you to begin again at the beginning with the nominatives." Bur-Malottke swore, but his curses were silent ones which only he could hear, for Murke had disconnected him and did not switch him on again until he had begun to say "that higher Being . . ." Murke was too young, considered himself too civilized, to approve of the word hate. But here, behind the glass pane, while Bur-Malottke repeated his genitives, he suddenly knew the meaning of hatred: he hated this great fat, handsome creature, whose books—two million three hundred and fifty thousand copies of them—lay around in libraries, bookstores, bookshelves and bookcases, and not for one second did he dream of suppressing this hatred. When Bur-Malottke had repeated two genitives, Murke switched on his own mike and said quietly: "Excuse me for interrupting you: the nominatives were excellent, so was the first genitive, but would you mind doing the second genitive again? Rather gentler in tone, rather more relaxed—I'll play it back to you." And although Bur-Malottke shook his head violently he signaled to the technician to play back the tape in the studio. They saw Bur-Malottke give a start, sweat more profusely than ever, then hold his hands over his ears until the tape came to an end. He said something, swore, but Murke and the technician could not hear him; they had disconnected him. Coldly Murke waited until he could read from Bur-Malottke's lips that he had begun again with the higher Being, he turned on the mike and the tape, and Bur-Malottke continued with the genitives.

When he was through, he screwed up Murke's list into a ball, rose from his chair, drenched in sweat and fuming, and made for the door; but Murke's quiet, pleasant young voice called him back. Murke said: "But Professor, you've forgotten the vocative." Bur-Malottke looked at him, his eyes blazing with hate, and said into the mike: "O Thou higher Being Whom we revere!"

As he turned to leave, Murke's voice called him back once more. Murke said: "I'm sorry, Professor, but, spoken like that, the words are useless."

"For God's sake," whispered the technician, "watch it!" Bur-Malottke was standing stock-still by the door, his back to the glass booth, as if transfixed by Murke's voice.

Something had happened to him which had never happened to him before: he was helpless, and this young voice, so pleasant, so remarkably intelligent, tortured him as nothing had ever tortured him before. Murke went on:

"I can, of course, paste it into the talk the way it is, but I must point out to you, Professor, that it will have the wrong effect."

Bur-Malottke turned, walked back to the microphone, and said in low and solemn tones:

"O Thou higher Being Whom we revere."

Without turning to look at Murke, he left the studio. It was exactly quarter past ten, and in the doorway he collided with a young, pretty woman carrying some sheet music. The girl, a vivacious redhead, walked briskly to the microphone, adjusted it, and moved the table to one side so she could stand directly in front of the mike.

In the booth Murke chatted for half a minute with Huglieme, who was in charge of Light Entertainment. Pointing to the metal container, Huglieme said: "Do you still need that?" And Murke said, "Yes, I do." In the studio the redhead was singing, "Take my lips, just as they are, they're so lovely." Huglieme switched on his microphone and said quietly: "D'you mind keeping your trap shut for another twenty seconds, I'm not quite ready." The girl laughed, made a face, and said: "O.K., pansy dear." Murke said to the technician: "I'll be back at eleven; we can cut it up then and splice it all together."

"Will we have to hear it through again after that?" asked the technician. "No," said Murke, "I wouldn't listen to it again for a million marks."

The technician nodded, inserted the tape for the red-haired singer, and Murke left.

He put a cigarette between his lips, did not light it, and walked along the rear corridor toward the second paternoster, the one on the south side leading down to the coffee shop. The rugs, the corridors, the furniture and the pictures, everything irritated him. The rugs were impressive, the corridors were impressive, the furniture was impressive, and the pictures were in excellent taste, but he suddenly felt a desire to take the sentimental picture of the Sacred Heart which his mother had sent him and see it somewhere here on the wall. He stopped, looked round, listened, took the picture from his pocket and stuck it between the wallpaper and the frame of the door to the Assistant Drama Producer's office. The tawdry little print was highly colored, and beneath the picture of the Sacred Heart were the words: *I prayed for you at St. James' Church.*

Murke continued along the corridor, got into the paternoster, and was carried down. On this side of the building the Schrumsnot ashtrays, which had won a Good Design Award, had already been installed. They hung next to the illuminated red figures indicating the floor: a red four, a Schrumsnot ashtray, a red three, a Schrumsnot ashtray, a red two, a Schrumsnot ashtray. They were handsome ashtrays, scallop-shaped, made of beaten copper, the beaten copper base an exotic marine plant, nodular seaweed—and each ashtray had cost two hundred and fifty-eight marks and seventy-seven pfennigs. They were so handsome that Murke could never bring himself to soil them with cigarette ash, let alone anything as sordid as a butt. Other smokers all seemed to have had the same feeling—empty packs, butts and ash littered the floor under the handsome ashtrays: apparently no one had the courage to use them as ashtrays; they were copper, burnished, forever empty.

Murke saw the fifth ashtray next to the illuminated red zero rising toward him, the air was getting warmer, there was a smell of food. Murke jumped off and stumbled into the coffee shop. Three free-lance colleagues were sitting at a table in the corner. The table was covered with used plates, cups, and saucers.

The three men were the joint authors of a radio series, *The Lung, A Human Organ;* they had collected their fee together, breakfasted together, were having a drink together, and were now throwing dice for the expense voucher. One of them, Wendrich, Murke knew well, but just then Wendrich shouted: "Art!"—"art," he shouted again, "art, art!" and Murke felt a spasm, like the frog when Galvani discovered electricity. The last two days Murke had heard the word *art* too often, from Bur-Malottke's lips; it occurred exactly one hundred and thirty-four times in the two talks; and he had heard the talks three times, which meant he had heard the word *art* four hundred and two times, too often to feel any desire to discuss it. He squeezed past the counter toward a booth in the far corner and was relieved to find it empty. He sat down, lit his cigarette, and when Wulla, the waitress, came, he said: "Apple juice, please," and was glad when Wulla went off again at once. He closed his eyes tight, but found himself listening willy-nilly to the conversation of the free-lance writers over in the corner, who seemed to be having a heated argument about art; each time one of them shouted "art" Murke winced. It's like being whipped, he thought.

As she brought him the apple juice Wulla looked at him in concern. She was tall and strongly built, but not fat, she had a healthy, cheerful face, and as she poured the apple juice from the jug into the glass she said:

"You ought to take a vacation, sir, and quit smoking."

She used to call herself Wilfriede-Ulla, but later, for the sake of simplicity, she combined the names into Wulla. She especially admired the people from the Cultural Department.

"Lay off, will you?" said Murke, "please!"

"And you ought to take some nice ordinary girl to the movies one night," said Wulla.

"I'll do that this evening," said Murke, "I promise you."

"It doesn't have to be one of those dolls," said Wulla, "just some nice, quiet, ordinary girl, with a kind heart. There are still some of those around."

"Yes," said Murke, "I know they're still around, as a matter of fact I know one." Well, that's fine then, thought Wulla, and went over to the free lances, one of whom had ordered three drinks and three coffees. Poor fellows, thought Wulla, art will be the death of them yet. She had a soft spot for the free lances and was always trying to persuade them to economize. The minute they have any money, she thought, they blow it; she went up to the counter and, shaking her head, passed on the order for the three drinks and the three coffees.

Murke drank some of the apple juice, stubbed out his cigarette in the ashtray, and thought with apprehension of the hours from eleven to one when he had to cut up Bur-Malottke's sentences and paste them into the right places in the talks. At two o'clock the Director wanted both talks played back to him in his studio. Murke thought about soap, about staircases, steep stairs and roller coasters, he thought about the dynamic personality of the Director, he thought about Bur-Malottke, and was startled by the sight of Schwendling coming into the coffee shop.

Schwendling had on a shirt of large red and black checks and made a beeline for the booth where Murke was hiding. Schwendling was humming the tune which was very popular just then: "Take my lips, just as they are, they're so lovely. . . ." He stopped short when he saw Murke, and said: "Hullo, you here? I thought you were busy carving up that crap of Bur-Malottke's."

"I'm going back at eleven," said Murke.

"Wulla, let's have some beer," shouted Schwendling over to the counter, "a pint. Well," he said to Murke, "you deserve extra time off for that, it must be a filthy job. The old man told me all about it."

Murke said nothing, and Schwendling went on:

"Have you heard the latest about Muckwitz?"

Murke, not interested, first shook his head, then for politeness' sake asked: "What's he been up to?"

Wulla brought the beer, Schwendling swallowed some, paused for effect, and announced: "Muckwitz is doing a feature about the Steppes."

Murke laughed and said: "What's Fenn doing?"

"Fenn," said Schwendling, "Fenn's doing a feature about the Tundra."

"And Weggucht?"

"Weggucht is doing a feature about me, and after that I'm going to do a feature about him, you know the old saying: You feature me, I'll feature you. . . ."

Just then one of the free lances jumped up and shouted across the room: "Art—art—that's the only thing that matters!"

Murke ducked, like a soldier when he hears the mortars being fired from the enemy trenches. He swallowed another mouthful of apple juice and winced again when a voice over the loudspeaker said: "Mr. Murke is wanted in Studio Thirteen—Mr. Murke is wanted in Studio Thirteen." He looked at his watch, it was only half-past ten, but the voice went on relentlessly: "Mr. Murke is wanted in Studio Thirteen—Mr. Murke is wanted in Studio Thirteen." The loudspeaker hung above the counter, immediately below the motto the Director had had painted on the wall: *Discipline Above All.*

"Well," said Schwendling, "that's it, you'd better go."

"Yes," said Murke, "that's it."

He got up, put money for the apple juice on the table, pressed past the free lances' table, got into the paternoster outside and was carried up once more past the five Schrumsnot ashtrays. He saw his Sacred Heart picture still sticking in the Assistant Producer's doorframe and thought:

"Thank God, now there's at least one corny picture in this place."

He opened the door of the studio booth, saw the technician sitting alone and relaxed in front of three cardboard boxes, and asked wearily: "What's up?"

"They were ready sooner than expected, and we've got an extra half hour in hand," said the technician. "I thought you'd be glad of the extra time."

"I certainly am," said Murke, "I've got an appointment at one. Let's get on with it then. What's the idea of the boxes?"

"Well," said the technician, "for each grammatical case I've got one box—the nominatives in the first, the genitives in the second, and in that one—" he pointed to the little box on the right with the words "Pure Chocolate" on it, and said: "in that one I have the two vocatives, the good one in the right-hand corner, the bad one in the left."

"That's terrific," said Murke, "so you've already cut up the crap."

"That's right," said the technician, "and if you've made a note of the order in which the cases have to be spliced it won't take us more than an hour. Did you write it down?"

"Yes, I did," said Murke. He pulled a piece of paper from his pocket with the numbers 1 to 27; each number was followed by a grammatical case.

Murke sat down, held out his cigarette pack to the technician; they both smoked while the technician laid the cut tapes with Bur-Malottke's talks on the roll.

"In the first cut," said Murke, "we have to stick in a nominative."

The technician put his hand into the first box, picked up one of the snippets and stuck it into the space.

"Next comes a genitive," said Murke.

They worked swiftly, and Murke was relieved that it all went so fast.

"Now," he said, "comes the vocative; we'll take the bad one, of course."

The technician laughed and stuck Bur-Malottke's bad vocative into the tape.

"Next," he said, "next!" "Genitive," said Murke.

The Director conscientiously read every listener's letter. The one he was reading at this particular moment went as follows:

Dear Radio,

I am sure you can have no more faithful listener than myself. I am an old woman, a little old lady of seventy-seven, and I have been listening to you every day for thirty years. I have never been sparing with my praise. Perhaps you remember my letter about the program: "The Seven Souls of Kaweida the Cow." It was a lovely program—but now I have to be angry with you! The way the canine soul is being neglected in radio is gradually becoming a disgrace. And you call that humanism. I am sure Hitler had his bad points: if one is to believe all one hears, he was a dreadful man, but one thing he did have: a real affection for dogs, and he did a lot for them. When are dogs going to come into their own again in German radio? The way you tried to do it in the program "Like Cat and Dog" is certainly not the right one: it was an insult to every canine soul. If my little Lohengrin could only talk, he'd tell you! And the way he barked, poor darling, all through your terrible program, it almost made me die of shame. I pay my two marks a month like any other listener and stand on my rights and demand to know: When are dogs going to come into their own again in German radio?

With kind regards—in spite of my being so cross with you,

Sincerely yours,
Jadwiga Herchen (retired)

P.S. In case none of those cynics of yours who run your programs should be capable of doing justice to the canine soul, I suggest you make use of my modest attempts, which are enclosed herewith. I do not wish to accept any fee. You may send it direct to the S.P.C.A. Enclosed: 35 manuscripts.

Yours,
J.H.

The Director sighed. He looked for the scripts, but his secretary had evidently filed them away. The Director filled his pipe, lit it, ran his tongue over his dynamic lips, lifted the receiver and asked to be put through to Krochy. Krochy had a tiny office with a tiny desk, although in the best of taste, upstairs in Culture and was in charge of a section as narrow as his desk: Animals in the World of Culture.

"Krochy speaking," he said diffidently into the telephone.

"Say, Krochy," said the Director, "when was the last time we had a program about dogs?"

"Dogs, sir?" said Krochy. "I don't believe we ever have, at least not since I've been here."

"And how long have you been here, Krochy?" And upstairs in his office Krochy trembled, because the Director's voice was so gentle; he knew it boded no good when that voice became gentle.

"I've been here ten years now, sir," said Krochy.

"It's a disgrace," said the Director, "that you've never had a program about dogs; after all, that's your department. What was the title of your last program?"

"The title of my last program was—" stammered Krochy.

"You don't have to repeat every sentence," said the Director, "we're not in the army."

"Owls in the Ruins," said Krochy timidly.

"Within the next three weeks," said the Director, gentle again now, "I would like to hear a program about the canine soul."

"Certainly, sir," said Krochy; he heard the click as the Director put down the receiver, sighed deeply and said: "Oh God!"

The Director picked up the next listener's letter.

At this moment Bur-Malottke entered the room. He was always at liberty to enter unannounced, and he made frequent use of this liberty. He was still sweating as he sank wearily into a chair opposite the Director and said:

"Well, good morning."

"Good morning," said the Director, pushing the listener's letter aside. "What can I do for you?"

"Could you give me one minute?"

"Bur-Malottke," said the Director, with a generous,

dynamic gesture, "does not have to ask me for one minute; hours, days, are at your disposal."

"No," said Bur-Malottke, "I don't mean an ordinary minute, I mean one minute of radio time. Due to the changes my talk has become one minute longer."

The Director grew serious, like a satrap distributing provinces. "I hope," he said, sourly, "it's not a political minute."

"No," said Bur-Malottke, "it's half a minute of Neighborly News and half a minute of Light Entertainment."

"Thank God for that," said the Director. "I've got a credit of seventy-nine seconds with Light Entertainment and eighty-three seconds with Neighborly News. I'll be glad to let someone like Bur-Malottke have one minute."

"I am overcome," said Bur-Malottke.

"Is there anything else I can do for you?" asked the Director.

"I would appreciate it," said Bur-Malottke, "if we could gradually start correcting all the tapes I have made since 1945. One day," he said—he passed his hand over his forehead and gazed wistfully at the genuine Kokoschka above the Director's desk—"one day I shall—" he faltered, for the news he was about to break to the Director was too painful for posterity "—one day I shall—die," and he paused again, giving the Director a chance to look gravely shocked and raise his hand in protest, "and I cannot bear the thought that after my death tapes may be run off on which I say things I no longer believe in. Particularly in some of my political utterances, during the fervor of 1945, I let myself be persuaded to make statements which today fill me with serious misgivings and which I can only account for on the basis of that spirit of youthfulness which has always distinguished my work. My written works are already in process of being corrected, and I would like to ask you to give me the opportunity of correcting my spoken works as well."

The Director was silent, he cleared his throat slightly, and little shining beads of sweat appeared on his forehead: it occurred to him that Bur-Malottke had spoken for at least an hour every month since 1945, and he made a swift calculation while Bur-Malottke went on talking: twelve times ten hours meant one hundred and twenty hours of spoken Bur-Malottke.

"Pedantry," Bur-Malottke was saying, "is something that only impure spirits regard as unworthy of genius; we know, of course"—and the Director felt flattered to be ranked by the We among the pure spirits—"that the true geniuses, the great geniuses, were pedants. Himmelsheim once had a whole printed edition of his *Seelon* rebound at his own expense because he felt that three or four sentences in the central portion of the work were no longer appropriate. The idea that some of my talks might be broadcast which no longer correspond to my convictions when I depart this earthly life—I find such an idea intolerable. How do you propose we go about it?"

The beads of sweat on the Director's forehead had become larger. "First of all," he said in a subdued voice, "an exact list would have to be made of all your broadcast talks, and then we would have to check in the archives to see if all the tapes were still there."

"I should hope," said Bur-Malottke, "that none of the tapes has been erased without notifying me. I have not been notified, therefore no tapes have been erased."

"I will see to everything," said the Director.

"Please do," said Bur-Malottke curtly, and rose from his chair. "Good-by."

"Good-by," said the Director, as he accompanied Bur-Malottke to the door.

The free lances in the coffee shop had decided to order lunch. They had had some more drinks, they were still talking about art, their conversation was quieter now but no less intense. They all jumped to their feet when Wanderburn suddenly came in. Wanderburn was a tall, despondent-looking writer with dark hair, an attractive face somewhat etched by the stigma of fame. On this particular morning he had not shaved, which made him look even more attractive. He walked over to the table where the three free lances were sitting, sank exhausted into a chair and said: "For God's sake, give me a drink. I always have the feeling in this building that I'm dying of thirst."

They passed him a drink, a glass that was still standing on the table, and the remains of a bottle of soda water. Wanderburn swallowed the drink, put down his glass, looked at each of the three men in turn, and said: "I must warn you about the radio business, about this pile of junk—this immaculate, shiny, slippery pile of junk. I'm warning you. It'll destroy us all." His warning was sincere and impressed the three young men very much; but the three young men did not know that Wanderburn had just come from the accounting department where he had picked up a nice fat fee for a quick job of editing the Book of Job.

"They cut us," said Wanderburn, "they consume our substance, splice us together again, and it'll be more than any of us can stand."

He finished the soda water, put the glass down on the table and, his coat flapping despondently about him, strode to the door.

On the dot of noon Murke finished the splicing. They had just stuck in the last snippet, a genitive, when Murke got up. He already had his hand on the doorknob when the technician said: "I wish I could afford a sensitive and expensive conscience like that. What'll we do with the box?" He pointed to the flat tin lying on the shelf next to the cardboard boxes containing the new tapes.

"Just leave it there," said Murke.

"What for?"

"We might need it again."

"D'you think he might get pangs of conscience all over again?"

"He might," said Murke, "we'd better wait and see. So long." He walked to the front paternoster, rode down to the second floor, and for the first time that day entered his office. His secretary had gone to lunch; Murke's boss, Humkoke, was sitting by the phone reading a book. He smiled at Murke, got up and said: "Well, I see you survived. Is this your book? Did you put it on the desk?" He held it out for Murke to read the title, and Murke said: "Yes, that's mine." The book had a jacket of green, gray and orange and was called "Batley's Lyrics of the Gutter"; it was about a young English writer a hundred years ago who had drawn up a catalogue of London slang.

"It's a marvelous book," said Murke.

"Yes," said Humkoke, "it is marvelous, but you never learn."

Murke eyed him questioningly.

"You never learn that one doesn't leave marvelous books lying around when Wanderburn is liable to turn up, and Wanderburn is always liable to turn up. He saw it at once, of course, opened it, read it for five minutes, and what's the result?"

Murke said nothing.

"The result," said Humkoke, "is two hour-long broadcasts by Wanderburn on 'Lyrics of the Gutter.' One day this fellow will do a feature about his own grandmother, and the worst of it is that one of his grandmothers was one of mine too. Please, Murke, try and remember: never leave marvelous books around when Wanderburn is liable to turn up, and, I repeat, he's always liable to turn up. That's all, you can go now, you've got the afternoon off, and I'm sure you've earned it. Is the stuff ready? Did you hear it through again?"

"It's all done," said Murke, "but I can't hear the talks through again, I simply can't."

" 'I simply can't' is a very childish thing to say," said Humkoke.

"If I have to hear the word Art one more time today I shall become hysterical," said Murke.

"You already are," said Humkoke, "and I must say you've every reason to be. Three hours of Bur-Malottke, that's too much for anybody, even the toughest of us, and you're not even tough." He threw the book on the table, took a step toward Murke and said: "When I was your age I once had to cut three minutes out of a four-hour speech of Hitler's, and I had to listen to the speech three times before I was considered worthy of suggesting which three minutes should be cut. When I began listening to the tape for the first time I was still a Nazi, but by the time I had heard the speech for the third time I wasn't a Nazi any more; it was a drastic cure, a terrible one, but very effective."

"You forget," said Murke quietly, "that I had already been cured of Bur-Malottke before I had to listen to his tapes."

"You really are a vicious beast!" said Humkoke with a laugh. "That'll do for now, the Director is going to hear it through again at two. Just see that you're available in case anything goes wrong."

"I'll be at home from two to three," said Murke.

"One more thing," said Humkoke, pulling out a yellow biscuit tin from a shelf next to Murke's desk, "what's this scrap you've got here?"

Murke colored. "It's—" he stammered, "I collect a certain kind of left-overs."

"What kind of left-overs?" asked Humkoke.

"Silences," said Murke, "I collect silences."

Humkoke raised his eyebrows, and Murke went on: "When I have to cut tapes, in the places where the speakers sometimes pause for a moment—or sigh, or take a breath, or there is absolute silence—I don't throw that away, I collect it. Incidentally, there wasn't a single second of silence in Bur-Malottke's tapes."

Humkoke laughed: "Of course not, he would never be silent. And what do you do with the scrap?"

"I splice it together and play back the tape when I'm at home in the evening. There's not much yet, I only have three minutes so far—but then people aren't silent very often."

"You know, don't you, that it's against regulations to take home sections of tape?"

"Even silences?" asked Murke.

Humkoke laughed and said: "For God's sake, get out!" And Murke left.

When the Director entered his studio a few minutes after two, the Bur-Malottke tape had just been turned on:

> . . . and wherever, however, why ever, and whenever we begin to discuss the Nature of Art, we must first look to that higher Being Whom we revere, we must bow in awe before that higher Being Whom we revere, and we must accept Art as a gift from that higher Being Whom we revere. Art . . . .

No, thought the Director, I really can't ask anyone to listen to Bur-Malottke for a hundred and twenty hours. No, he thought, there are some things one simply cannot do, things I wouldn't want to wish even on Murke. He returned to his office and switched on the loudspeaker just in time to hear Bur-Malottke say: "O Thou higher Being Whom we revere. . . ." No, thought the Director, no, no.

Murke lay on his chesterfield at home smoking. Next to him on a chair was a cup of tea, and Murke was gazing at the white ceiling of the room. Sitting at his desk was a very pretty blonde who was staring out of the window at the street. Between Murke and the girl, on a low coffee table, stood a tape recorder, recording. Not a word was spoken, not a sound was made. The girl was pretty and silent enough for a photographer's model.

"I can't stand it," said the girl suddenly, "I can't stand it, it's inhuman, what you want me to do. There are some men who expect a girl to do immoral things, but it seems to me that what you are asking me to do is even more immoral than the things other men expect a girl to do."

Murke sighed. "Oh hell," he said, "Rina dear, now I've got to cut all that out; do be sensible, be a good girl and put just five more minutes' silence on the tape."

"Put silence," said the girl, with what thirty years ago would have been called a pout. "Put silence, that's another of your inventions. I wouldn't mind putting words onto a tape—but putting silence. . . ."

Murke had got up and switched off the tape recorder. "Oh Rina," he said, "if you only knew how precious your silence is to me. In the evening, when I'm tired, when I'm sitting here alone, I play back your silence. Do be a dear and put just three more minutes' silence on the tape for me and save me the cutting; you know how I feel about cutting." "Oh all right," said the girl, "but give me a cigarette at least."

Murke smiled, gave her a cigarette and said: "This way I have your silence in the original and on tape, that's terrific." He switched the tape on again, and they sat facing one another in silence till the telephone rang. Murke got up, shrugged helplessly, and lifted the receiver.

"Well," said Humkoke, "the tapes ran off smoothly, the boss couldn't find a thing wrong with them. . . . You can go to the movies now. And think about snow."

"What snow?" asked Murke, looking out onto the street, which lay basking in brilliant summer sunshine.

"Come on now," said Humkoke, "you know we have to start thinking about the winter programs. I need songs about snow, stories about snow—we can't fool around for the rest of our lives with Schubert and Stifter. No one seems to have any idea how badly we need snow songs and snow stories. Just imagine if we have a long hard winter with lots of snow and freezing temperatures: where are we going to get our snow programs from? Try and think of something snowy."

"All right," said Murke, "I'll try and think of something." Humkoke had hung up.

"Come along," he said to the girl, "we can go to the movies."

"May I speak again now?" said the girl.

"Yes," said Murke, "speak!"

It was just at this time that the Assistant Drama Producer had finished listening again to the one-act play scheduled for that evening. He liked it, only the ending did not satisfy him. He was sitting in the glass booth in Studio Thirteen next to the technician, chewing a match and studying the script.

(*Sound-effects of a large empty church*)

ATHEIST: (*in a loud clear voice*) Who will remember me when I have become the prey of worms?

(*Silence*)

ATHEIST: (*his voice a shade louder*) Who will wait for me when I have turned into dust?

(*Silence*)

ATHEIST: (*louder still*) And who will remember me when I have turned into leaves?

(*Silence*)

There were twelve such questions called out by the atheist into the church, and each question was followed by—? Silence.

The Assistant Producer removed the chewed match from his lips, replaced it with a fresh one and looked at the technician, a question in his eyes.

"Yes," said the technician, "if you ask me: I think there's a bit too much silence in it."

"That's what I thought," said the Assistant Producer; "the author thinks so too and he's given me leave to change it. There should just be a voice saying: "God" —but it ought to be a voice without church sound-effects, it would have to be spoken somehow in a different acoustical environment. Have you any idea where I can get hold of a voice like that at this hour?"

The technician smiled, picked up the metal container which was still lying on the shelf. "Here you are," he said, "here's a voice saying 'God' without any sound-effects."

The Assistant Producer was so surprised he almost swallowed the match, choked a little and got it up into the front of his mouth again. "It's quite all right," the technician said with a smile, "we had to cut it out of a talk, twenty-seven times."

"I don't need it that often, just twelve times," said the Assistant Producer.

"It's a simple matter, of course," said the technician, "to cut out the silence and stick in God twelve times—if you'll take the responsibility."

"You're a godsend," said the Assistant Producer, "and I'll be responsible. Come on, let's get started." He gazed happily at the tiny, lusterless tape snippets in Murke's tin box. "You really are a godsend," he said, "come on, let's go!"

The technician smiled, for he was looking forward to being able to present Murke with the snippets of silence: it was a lot of silence, altogether nearly a minute;

it was more silence than he had ever been able to give Murke, and he liked the young man.

"O.K.," he said with a smile, "here we go."

The Assistant Producer put his hand in his jacket pocket, took out a pack of cigarettes; in doing so he touched a crumpled piece of paper, he smoothed it out and passed it to the technician: "Funny, isn't it, the corny stuff you can come across in this place? I found this stuck in my door."

The technician took the picture, looked at it, and said: "Yes, it's funny," and he read out the words under the picture:

I prayed for you at St. James' Church.

Bonn diary

Monday

Unfortunately I arrived too late to go out again or pay any calls; it was 2330 hours when I got to the hotel, and I was tired. So I had to be satisfied with looking out of the hotel window at the city lying there scintillating with life—bubbling, throbbing, boiling over, one might say: there are vital forces hidden there just waiting to be released. The city is still not all it might be. I smoked a cigar, abandoning myself wholly to this fascinating electric energy; I wondered whether I should phone Inna, finally resigned myself with a sigh and had one more look through my important files. Toward midnight I went to bed: I always find it hard to go to bed here. This city is not conducive to sleep.

Night jottings

Strange dream, very strange: I was walking through a forest of monuments, straight rows of them; in little clearings there were miniature parks, each with a monument in the center; all the monuments were alike, hundreds, thousands of them: a man standing "at ease," an officer to judge by the creases in his soft boots, yet the chest, face and pedestal of each monument were covered with a cloth—suddenly all the monuments were unveiled simultaneously, and I realized, without any particular surprise, that *I* was the man standing on the pedestal; I shifted my position on the pedestal, smiled, and now that the covering had dropped off I could read my name thousands of times over: *Erich von Machorka-Muff. I* laughed, and the laugh echoed back to me a thousand times from my own mouth.

Tuesday

Filled with a deep sense of happiness, I fell asleep again, woke refreshed, and laughed as I looked at my-self in the mirror: it is only here in the capital that one has dreams like that. Before I had finished shaving, the first call from Inna. (That's what I call my old friend Inniga von Schekel-Pehnunz, a member of the new no-bility but an old family: her father, Ernst von Schekel, was raised to the aristocracy by Wilhelm II only two days before the latter abdicated, but I have no qualms about regarding Inna as a friend of equal rank.)

On the phone Inna was—as always—sweet, managed to squeeze in some gossip and in her own way gave me to understand that the project which was the main reason for my visit to the capital was coming along very well. "The corn is ripe," she said softly, and then, barely pausing: "The baby's being christened today." She hung up quickly, to prevent me from asking questions in my impatience. Deep in thought I went down to the breakfast room: had she really meant the laying of the foundation stone? My frank, forthright soldierly nature still has difficulty understanding Inna's cryptic remarks.

Again in the breakfast room this abundance of virile faces, most of them well-bred: I passed the time by imagining which man would be suitable for which post, an old habit of mine; before I had even shelled my egg I had already found first-rate material for two regimental staffs and one divisional staff, and there were still some candidates left over for the general staff; playing games in my head, so to speak—just the thing for a veteran observer of human nature like myself. The memory of my dream enhanced my pleasant mood: strange, to walk through a forest of monuments and to see oneself on every pedestal. I wonder whether the psychologists have really plumbed all the depths of the self?

I ordered my coffee to be brought to the lobby, smoked a cigar and observed the time with a smile: 0956 hours—would Heffling be punctual? I had not seen him for six years, we had corresponded occasionally (the usual exchange of post cards one has with inferiors in the ranks).

I actually found myself feeling nervous about Heffling's punctuality; the trouble with me is, I am inclined to regard everything as symptomatic: Heffling's punctuality became for me the punctuality *per se* of the ranks. I remembered with a touch of emotion what my old divisional chief, Welk von Schnomm, used to say: "Macho, you are and always will be an idealist."

(Memo: renew the standing order for upkeep of Schnomm's grave.)

Am I an idealist? I fell into a reverie, until Heffling's voice roused me: I looked first at the time—two minutes after ten (I have always allowed him this microscopic reserve of privilege)—then at him: how fat the fellow's got, grossly fat around the neck, hair getting thin, but still that phallic sparkle in his eyes, and his "Present, Colonel!" sounded just like old times. "Heffling!" I cried, slapping him on the shoulder and ordering a double schnapps for him. He stood at attention as he took the drink from the waiter's tray; I drew him by the sleeve over to the corner, and we were soon deep in reminiscences: "Remember the time at Schwichi-Schwaloche, the ninth . . . ?"

It is heart-warming to observe how powerless the vagaries of fashion are to corrode the wholesome spirit of the people: the homespun virtues, the hearty male laugh, and the never-failing readiness to share a good dirty story, are still to be found. While Heffling was telling me some variations of the familiar subject in an undertone, I noticed Murcks-Maloche had entered the lobby and—without speaking to me, as arranged—had disappeared into the rear of the restaurant. By a glance at my wristwatch I indicated to Heffling that I was pressed for time, and with the sound instincts of the simple man he understood immediately that he had to leave. "Come and see us some time, Colonel, my wife would be delighted." Laughing and joking we walked side by side to the porter's desk, and I promised Heffling I would come and see him. Perhaps an opportunity would offer for a little adventure with his wife; every now and again I feel the urge to partake of the husky eroticism of the lower classes, and one never knows what arrows Cupid may be holding in store in his quiver.

I sat down beside Murcks, ordered some Hennessy and, as soon as the waiter had gone, said in my straightforward fashion:

"Well, fire away."

"Yes, we've made it." He laid his hand on mine and whispered: "I'm so glad, Macho, so glad."

"I'm pleased too," I said warmly, "that one of the dreams of my youth has come to pass. And in a democracy too."

"A democracy in which we have the majority of Parliament on our side is a great deal better than a dictatorship."

I felt constrained to stand up; I was filled with solemn pride; historic moments have always moved me deeply.

"Murcks," I said, choking back the tears, "is it really true then?"

"It's true, Macho," he said.

"It's all settled?"

"It's all settled—you're to give the dedication address today. The first course of instruction is starting right away. Those enrolled are still being put up in hotels, till the project can be officially declared open."

"Will the public—will it swallow it?"

"It'll swallow it—the public will swallow anything," said Murcks.

"On your feet, Murcks," I said, "let's drink a toast, let's drink to the spirit to which this building is dedicated: to the spirit of military memories."

We clinked glasses and drank.

I was too moved to undertake any serious business that morning; I went restlessly up to my room, from there to the lobby, wandered through this enchanting city, after Murcks had driven off to the Ministry. Although I was in civilians, I had the impression of a sword dangling at my side; there are some sensations which are really only appropriate when one is in uniform. Once again, while I was strolling through the city, looking forward to my tête-à-tête with Inna, uplifted by the certainty that my plan had become reality—once again I had every reason to recall one of Schnomm's expressions: "Macho, Macho," he used to say, "you've always got your head in the clouds." He had said it when there were only thirteen men left in my regiment and I had four of those men shot for mutiny.

In honor of the occasion I permitted myself an apéritif at a café not far from the station; I looked through some newspapers, glanced at a few editorials on defense policy, and tried to imagine what Schnomm—if he were still alive—would have said had he read the articles. "Those Christians—" he would have said, "who would have thought it of them!"

At last it was time to go to the hotel and change for my rendezvous with Inna: her signal on the car horn—a Beethoven motif—made me look out of the window; she waved up at me from her lemon-yellow car: lemon-yellow hair, lemon-yellow dress, black gloves. With a sigh, after blowing her a kiss, I went to the mirror, tied my tie, and went downstairs; Inna would be the right wife for me, but she has been divorced seven times and, not unnaturally, is skeptical about the institution of marriage; besides, we are separated by a deep gulf in background and outlook: she comes from a strict Protestant family, I from a strict Catholic one—all the same, numbers link us together symbolically: she has been divorced seven times, I have been wounded seven times. Inna!! I still can't quite get used to being kissed on the street. . . .

Inna woke me at 1617 hours: she had some strong tea and ginger biscuits ready, and we quickly went once more through the files on Hürlanger-Hiss, the unforgotten field marshal to whose memory we planned to dedicate the building.

While I was examining the Hürlanger files once more, my arm around Inna's shoulder, lost in daydreams of her gift of love, I heard the band music: melancholy overtook me, for, like all the other experiences of this day, to listen to this music in civilian clothes was truly an ordeal.

The band music and Inna's nearness diverted my attention from the files; however, Inna had filled me in verbally so that I was fully equipped to give my speech. The doorbell rang as Inna was pouring out my second cup of tea; I jumped, but Inna smiled reassuringly. "An important guest," she said, returning from the hall, "a

guest whom we cannot possibly receive in here." There
was a twinkle in her eye as she gestured toward the
rumpled bed in all its delightful disarray of love. "Come
along," she said. I got out of bed, followed her in a kind
of daze, and was genuinely surprised to find myself face
to face in her living room with the Minister of Defense.
His frank, rugged countenance was shining. "General
von Machorka-Muff," he said, with a beaming smile,
"welcome to the capital!"

I could not believe my ears. With a twinkle in his eye
the Minister handed me my commission.

I think, looking back, I must have swayed for a moment and suppressed a few tears; but actually I am not
quite sure what was going on inside me; all I remember
is hearing myself say: "But Your Excellency—the
uniform—half an hour before the ceremony starts. . . ."
With a twinkle in his eye—what an admirable man he is,
what sterling qualities!—he glanced at Inna, Inna twin-
kled back at him, drew aside a chintz curtain dividing
off one corner of the room, and there it was, there hung
my uniform, with all my decorations on it. . . . Events,
emotions followed so thick and fast that looking back all
I can do is give their sequence in note-form:

We offered the Minister some refreshment and he had
a glass of beer while I changed in Inna's room.

Drive to the building site, which I was viewing for
the first time: I was extraordinarily moved by the sight
of this piece of land on which my pet project is to become
reality: the Academy for Military Memoirs, where every
veteran from the rank of major up is to be given the

opportunity of committing his reminiscences to paper, through conversations with old comrades and cooperation with the Ministry's Department of Military History; my own feeling is that a six-week course should suffice, but Parliament is willing to subsidize a three-month course. I was also thinking of having a few healthy working-class girls housed in a special wing, to sweeten the evening leisure hours of the comrades who are plagued with memories. I have gone to a great deal of trouble to find appropriate inscriptions. The main wing is to bear in gold lettering the inscription: MEMORIA DEXTERA EST; while over the girls' wing, which will also contain the bathrooms, will be the words: BALNEUM ET AMOR MARTIS DECOR. However, on the way there the Minister hinted that I should not mention this part of my plan just yet; he was afraid—perhaps rightly so—of opposition from some of his fellow members of Parliament, although—as he put it with a chuckle—no one could complain of lack of liberalization!

There were flags all around the building site, the band was playing: *I used to have a comrade,* as I walked beside the Minister toward the platform. Since with his usual modesty the Minister declined to open proceedings, I stepped up at once onto the dais, surveyed the row of assembled comrades, and, encouraged by a wink from Inna, began to speak:

"Your Excellency, comrades! This building, which is to bear the name Hürlanger-Hiss Academy for Military Memoirs, needs no justification. But a justification is required for the name Hürlanger-Hiss, a name which for many years—to this very day, I would say—has been regarded as dishonored. You all know the disgrace attaching to this name: when the army of Field Marshal Emil von Hürlanger-Hiss was obliged to retreat at Schwichi-Schwaloche, Hürlanger-Hiss could report a loss of only 8,500 men. According to the calculations of Tapir's specialists in retreat—Tapir, as you know, was our private name for Hitler—his army should, with the proper fighting spirit, have had a loss of 12,300 men. You are also aware, Your Excellency and comrades, of the insulting treatment to which Hürlanger-Hiss was subjected: he was transferred in disgrace to Biarritz, where he died of lobster poisoning. For years—a total of fourteen years—this dishonor has attached to his name. All the data on Hürlanger's army fell into the hands of Tapir's underlings, later into the hands of the Allies, but today, today," I cried, pausing so as to let my next words sink in, "today it can be taken as a proven fact, and I am prepared to make the material public, it can be taken as proven fact that our great Field Marshal's army suffered losses at Schwichi-Schwaloche of a total of 14,700 men: it can therefore be assumed beyond any doubt that his army fought with unexampled courage, and his name is now cleared of all blemish."

While I let the deafening applause pour over me and modestly diverted the ovation from myself to the Minister, I had a chance to observe from the faces of my comrades that they too were surprised by this information; how discreetly Inna had carried on her research!

To the strains of *See'st thou the dawn in eastern skies*
I took the trowel and stone from the mason and set the
cornerstone in place; it contained a photograph of
Hürlanger-Hiss together with one of his shoulder-straps.

At the head of my comrades I marched from the
building site to the villa, "The Golden Shekel," which
Inna's family has put at our disposal until the academy
has been completed. Here we had a brisk round of
drinks, a word of thanks from the Minister, and a tele-
gram from the Chancellor was read out, before the social
hour began.

The social hour was opened by a concerto for seven
drums, played by seven former generals; with the consent of the composer, a captain with musical aspirations,
it was announced that it would be known as the
Hürlanger-Hiss Memorial Septet. The social hour was
an unqualified success: songs were sung, stories told,
confidences exchanged, old quarrels forgotten.

Wednesday

We had just an hour to get ready for the church service; in relaxed marching order we made our way just before 0730 hours to the cathedral. Inna stood beside me
in church, and I felt encouraged when she whispered
that she recognized a colonel as her second husband, a
lieutenant-colonel as her fifth, and a captain as her sixth.
"And your eighth," I whispered in her ear, "will be a
general." My mind was made up; Inna blushed; she did
not hesitate when after it was over I took her into the
vestry to introduce her to the prelate who had conducted

the service. "Indeed, my dear child," the priest said, after we had discussed the church's position, "since none of your former marriages was solemnized in church, there is no obstacle to you and General von Machorka-Muff having a church wedding."

It was under these auspices that we had breakfast, in a gay mood, à deux; Inna was elated, I had never seen her quite like that. "I always feel like this," she said, "when I am a bride." I ordered champagne.

We decided to keep our engagement a secret for the time being, but as a little celebration we drove up to the Petersberg, a lovely hill a few miles outside Bonn, where Inna's cousin, whose maiden name was Pelf, had invited us for lunch. Inna's cousin was adorable.

The afternoon and evening were devoted entirely to love, the night to sleep.

Thursday

I still can't quite get used to the idea that I am living and working here; it must be a dream! Gave my first lecture this morning: "Reminiscence as a Historical Duty."

Annoying interlude at midday. Murcks-Maloche came to see me at the villa on behalf of the Minister to report that the opposition had expressed itself dissatisfied with our academy project.

"Opposition?" I asked, "what's that?"

Murcks enlightened me. I was astounded. "Let's get this straight," I said impatiently, "do we have the majority or don't we?"

"We do," said Murcks.

"Well then," I said. Opposition—a strange word, I don't like it at all; it is such a grim reminder of times that I thought were over and done with.

Inna, when I told her at teatime about my annoyance, consoled me.

"Erich," she said, putting her little hand on my arm, "no one has ever opposed our family."

Action will be taken

An Action-Packed Story

Probably one of the strangest interludes in my life was
the time I spent as an employee in Alfred Wunsiedel's
factory. By nature I am inclined more to pensiveness
and inactivity than to work, but now and again prolonged financial difficulties compel me—for pensiveness
is no more profitable than inactivity—to take on a so-
called job. Finding myself once again at a low ebb of
this kind, I put myself in the hands of the employment
office and was sent with seven other fellow-sufferers to
Wunsiedel's factory, where we were to undergo an apti-
tude test.

The exterior of the factory was enough to arouse my
suspicions: the factory was built entirely of glass brick,
and my aversion to well-lit buildings and well-lit rooms
is as strong as my aversion to work. I became even more
suspicious when we were immediately served breakfast
in the well-lit, cheerful coffee shop: pretty waitresses
brought us eggs, coffee and toast, orange juice was
served in tastefully designed jugs, goldfish pressed their
bored faces against the sides of pale-green aquariums.

The waitresses were so cheerful that they appeared to be bursting with good cheer. Only a strong effort of will—so it seemed to me—restrained them from singing away all day long. They were as crammed with unsung songs as chickens with unlaid eggs.

Right away I realized something that my fellow-sufferers evidently failed to realize: that this breakfast was already part of the test; so I chewed away reverently, with the full appreciation of a person who knows he is supplying his body with valuable elements. I did something which normally no power on earth can make me do: I drank orange juice on an empty stomach, left the coffee and egg untouched, as well as most of the toast, got up, and paced up and down in the coffee shop, pregnant with action.

As a result I was the first to be ushered into the room where the questionnaires were spread out on attractive tables. The walls were done in a shade of green that would have summoned the word "delightful" to the lips of interior decoration enthusiasts. The room appeared to be empty, and yet I was so sure of being observed that I behaved as someone pregnant with action behaves when he believes himself unobserved: I ripped my pen impatiently from my pocket, unscrewed the top, sat down at the nearest table and pulled the questionnaire toward me, the way irritable customers snatch at the bill in a restaurant.

Question No. 1: Do you consider it right for a human being to possess only two arms, two legs, eyes, and ears?

Here for the first time I reaped the harvest of my pensive nature and wrote without hesitation: "Even four arms, legs and ears would not be adequate for my driving energy. Human beings are very poorly equipped."

Question No. 2: How many telephones can you handle at one time?

Here again the answer was as easy as simple arithmetic: "When there are only seven telephones," I wrote, "I get impatient; there have to be nine before I feel I am working to capacity."

Question No. 3: How do you spend your free time?

My answer: "I no longer acknowledge the term free time—on my fifteenth birthday I eliminated it from my vocabulary, for in the beginning was the act."

I got the job. Even with nine telephones I really didn't feel I was working to capacity. I shouted into the mouthpieces: "Take immediate action!" or: "Do something! —We must have some action—Action will be taken— Action has been taken—Action should be taken." But as a rule—for I felt this was in keeping with the tone of the place—I used the imperative.

Of considerable interest were the noon-hour breaks, when we consumed nutritious foods in an atmosphere of silent good cheer. Wunsiedel's factory was swarming with people who were obsessed with telling you the story of their lives, as indeed vigorous personalities are fond of doing. The story of their lives is more important to them than their lives, you have only to press a button, and immediately it is covered with spewed-out exploits.

Wunsiedel had a right-hand man called Broschek,

who had in turn made a name for himself by supporting seven children and a paralyzed wife by working night-shifts in his student days, and successfully carrying on four business agencies, besides which he had passed two examinations with honors in two years. When asked by reporters: "When do you sleep, Mr. Broscheck?" he had replied: "It's a crime to sleep!"

Wunsiedel's secretary had supported a paralyzed husband and four children by knitting, at the same time graduating in psychology and German history as well as breeding shepherd dogs, and she had become famous as a night-club singer where she was known as *Vamp Number Seven*.

Wunsiedel himself was one of those people who every morning, as they open their eyes, make up their minds to act. "I must act," they think as they briskly tie their bathrobe belts around them. "I must act," they think as they shave, triumphantly watching their beard hairs being washed away with the lather: these hirsute vestiges are the first daily sacrifices to their driving energy. The more intimate functions also give these people a sense of satisfaction: water swishes, paper is used. Action has been taken. Bread gets eaten, eggs are decapitated.

With Wunsiedel, the most trivial activity looked like action: the way he put on his hat, the way—quivering with energy—he buttoned up his overcoat, the kiss he gave his wife, everything was action.

When he arrived at his office he greeted his secretary with a cry of "Let's have some action!" And in ringing tones she would call back: "Action will be taken!"

Wunsiedel then went from department to department, calling out his cheerful: "Let's have some action!" Everyone would answer: "Action will be taken!" And I would call back to him too, with a radiant smile, when he looked into my office: "Action will be taken!"

Within a week I had increased the number of telephones on my desk to eleven, within two weeks to thirteen, and every morning on the streetcar I enjoyed thinking up new imperatives, or chasing the words *take action* through various tenses and modulations: for two whole days I kept saying the same sentence over and over again because I thought it sounded so marvelous: "Action ought to have been taken;" for another two days it was: "Such action ought not to have been taken."

So I was really beginning to feel I was working to capacity when there actually was some action. One Tuesday morning—I had hardly settled down at my desk—Wunsiedel rushed into my office crying his "Let's have some action!" But an inexplicable something in his face made me hesitate to reply, in a cheerful gay voice as the rules dictated: "Action will be taken!" I must have paused too long, for Wunsiedel, who seldom raised his voice, shouted at me: "Answer! Answer, you know the rules!" And I answered, under my breath, reluctantly, like a child who is forced to say: I am a naughty child. It was only by a great effort that I managed to bring out the sentence: "Action will be taken," and hardly had I uttered it when there really was some action: Wunsiedel dropped to the floor. As he fell he rolled over onto his side and lay right across the open doorway. I knew at once, and I confirmed it when I went slowly around my desk and approached the body on the floor: he was dead.

Shaking my head I stepped over Wunsiedel, walked slowly along the corridor to Broschek's office, and entered without knocking. Broschek was sitting at his desk, a telephone receiver in each hand, between his teeth a ballpoint pen with which he was making notes on a writing pad, while with his bare feet he was operating a knitting machine under the desk. In this way he helps to clothe his family. "We've had some action," I said in a low voice.

Broschek spat out the ballpoint pen, put down the two receivers, reluctantly detached his toes from the knitting machine.

"What action?" he asked.

"Wunsiedel is dead," I said.

"No," said Broschek.

"Yes," I said, "come and have a look!"

"No," said Broschek, "that's impossible," but he put on his slippers and followed me along the corridor.

"No," he said, when we stood beside Wunsiedel's corpse, "no, no!" I did not contradict him. I carefully turned Wunsiedel over onto his back, closed his eyes, and looked at him pensively.

I felt something like tenderness for him, and realized for the first time that I had never hated him. On his face was that expression which one sees on children who obstinately refuse to give up their faith in Santa Claus, even though the arguments of their playmates sound so convincing.

"No," said Broschek, "no."

"We must take action," I said quietly to Broschek.

"Yes," said Broschek, "we must take action."

Action was taken: Wunsiedel was buried, and I was delegated to carry a wreath of artificial roses behind his coffin, for I am equipped with not only a penchant for pensiveness and inactivity but also a face and figure that go extremely well with dark suits. Apparently as I walked along behind Wunsiedel's coffin carrying the wreath of artificial roses I looked superb. I received an offer from a fashionable firm of funeral directors to join their staff as a professional mourner. "You are a born mourner," said the manager, "your outfit would be provided by the firm. Your face—simply superb!"

I handed in my notice to Broschek, explaining that I had never really felt I was working to capacity there; that, in spite of the thirteen telephones, some of my talents were going to waste. As soon as my first professional appearance as a mourner was over I knew: This is where I belong, this is what I am cut out for.

Pensively I stand behind the coffin in the funeral chapel, holding a simple bouquet, while the organ plays Handel's *Largo*, a piece that does not receive nearly the respect it deserves. The cemetery café is my regular haunt; there I spend the intervals between my professional engagements, although sometimes I walk behind coffins which I have not been engaged to follow, I pay for flowers out of my own pocket and join the welfare worker who walks behind the coffin of some homeless person. From time to time I also visit Wunsiedel's grave, for after all I owe it to him that I discovered my true vocation, a vocation in which pensiveness is essential and inactivity my duty.

It was not till much later that I realized I had never bothered to find out what was being produced in Wunsiedel's factory. I expect it was soap.

The laugher

When someone asks me what business I am in, I am
seized with embarrassment: I blush and stammer, I who
am otherwise known as a man of poise. I envy people
who can say: I am a bricklayer. I envy barbers, book-
keepers and writers the simplicity of their avowal, for
all these professions speak for themselves and need no
lengthy explanation, while I am constrained to reply to
such questions: I am a laugher. An admission of this
kind demands another, since I have to answer the second
question: "Is that how you make your living?" truth-
fully with "Yes." I actually do make a living at my
laughing, and a good one too, for my laughing is—
commercially speaking—much in demand. I am a good
laugher, experienced, no one else laughs as well as I do,
no one else has such command of the fine points of my
art. For a long time, in order to avoid tiresome explana-
tions, I called myself an actor, but my talents in the field
of mime and elocution are so meager that I felt this
designation to be too far from the truth: I love the truth,
and the truth is: I am a laugher. I am neither a clown

nor a comedian. I do not make people gay, I portray gaiety: I laugh like a Roman emperor, or like a sensitive schoolboy, I am as much at home in the laughter of the seventeenth century as in that of the nineteenth, and when occasion demands I laugh my way through all the centuries, all classes of society, all categories of age: it is simply a skill which I have acquired, like the skill of being able to repair shoes. In my breast I harbor the laughter of America, the laughter of Africa, white, red, yellow laughter—and for the right fee I let it peal out in accordance with the director's requirements.

I have become indispensable; I laugh on records, I laugh on tape, and television directors treat me with respect. I laugh mournfully, moderately, hysterically; I laugh like a streetcar conductor or like a helper in the grocery business; laughter in the morning, laughter in the evening, nocturnal laughter and the laughter of twilight. In short: wherever and however laughter is required—I do it.

It need hardly be pointed out that a profession of this kind is tiring, especially as I have also—this is my specialty—mastered the art of infectious laughter; this has also made me indispensable to third- and fourth-rate comedians, who are scared—and with good reason—that their audiences will miss their punch lines, so I spend most evenings in night clubs as a kind of discreet claque, my job being to laugh infectiously during the weaker parts of the program. It has to be carefully timed: my hearty, boisterous laughter must not come too soon, but neither must it come too late, it must come just at the right spot: at the pre-arranged moment I burst out laughing, the whole audience roars with me, and the joke is saved.

But as for me, I drag myself exhausted to the checkroom, put on my overcoat, happy that I can go off duty at last. At home I usually find telegrams waiting for me: "Urgently require your laughter. Recording Tuesday," and a few hours later I am sitting in an overheated express train bemoaning my fate.

I need scarcely say that when I am off duty or on vacation I have little inclination to laugh: the cowhand is glad when he can forget the cow, the bricklayer when he can forget the mortar, and carpenters usually have doors at home which don't work or drawers which are hard to open. Confectioners like sour pickles, butchers like marzipan, and the baker prefers sausage to bread; bullfighters raise pigeons for a hobby, boxers turn pale when their children have nose-bleeds: I find all this quite natural, for I never laugh off duty. I am a very solemn person, and people consider me—perhaps rightly so—a pessimist.

During the first years of our married life, my wife would often say to me: "Do laugh!" but since then she has come to realize that I cannot grant her this wish. I am happy when I am free to relax my tense face muscles, my frayed spirit, in profound solemnity. Indeed, even other people's laughter gets on my nerves, since it reminds me too much of my profession. So our marriage is a quiet, peaceful one, because my wife has also forgotten how to laugh: now and again I catch her smiling, and

I smile too. We converse in low tones, for I detest the noise of the night clubs, the noise that sometimes fills the recording studios. People who do not know me think I am taciturn. Perhaps I am, because I have to open my mouth so often to laugh.

I go through life with an impassive expression, from time to time permitting myself a gentle smile, and I often wonder whether I have ever laughed. I think not. My brothers and sisters have always known me for a serious boy.

So I laugh in many different ways, but my own laughter I have never heard.

In the valley of the thundering hooves

The boy had not noticed that it was his turn. He was staring at the tiles on the floor dividing the side nave from the center nave: they were red and white, shaped like honeycomb cells, the red ones were speckled with white, the white with red; he could no longer distinguish the white from the red, the tiles ran together, and the dark lines of the cement joins became blurred, the floor swam before his eyes like a gravel path of red and white chips; the red dazzled, the white dazzled, the joins lay indistinctly over them like a soiled net.

"It's your turn," whispered a young woman next to him; he shook his head, made a vague gesture with his thumb toward the confessional, and the woman went ahead of him; for a moment the smell of lavender became stronger; then he heard murmuring, the scuffing sound of her shoes on the wooden step as she knelt down.

Sins, he thought, death, sins; and the intensity with which he suddenly desired the woman was torture; he had not even seen her face; a faint smell of lavender, a young voice, the sound of her high heels, light yet crisp, as she walked the four steps to the confessional; this rhythm of the heels, crisp yet light, was but a fragment of the eternal refrain which seethed in his ears for days and nights on end. In the evening he would lie awake, beside the open window, and hear them walking along outside on the cobblestones, on the asphalt sidewalk: shoes, heels, crisp, light, unsuspecting; he could hear voices, whispering, laughter under the chestnut trees. There were too many of them, and they were too beautiful: some of them opened their handbags; in the street-car, at the movie box office, on the store counter, they would leave their handbags lying open in cars, and he could see inside: lipsticks, handkerchiefs, loose change, crumpled bus tickets, packs of cigarettes, compacts. His eyes were still moving in torment back and forth over the tiles: this was a thorny path, and never-ending.

"It's your turn, you know," said a voice beside him, and he looked up. A little girl, red-cheeked and with black hair. He smiled at the child and waved her on too with his thumb. Her flat child's shoes had no rhythm. Whispering over there to the right. What had he confessed, when he was her age? I stole some cookies. I told lies. Disobedient. Didn't do my homework. I stole from the sugar jar, cake crumbs, wine glasses with the dregs from grownups' parties. Cigarette butts. I stole some cookies.

"It's your turn." This time he waved mechanically. Men's shoes. Whispering and the obtrusiveness of that faint no-smell smell.

Once again his glance fell on the red and white chips

of the aisle. His naked eyes hurt as acutely as his naked feet would have hurt on a rough gravel path. The feet of my eyes, he thought, wander round their mouths as if round red lakes. The hands of my eyes wander over their skin.

Sins, death and the insolent unobtrusiveness of that no-smell smell. If only there were someone who smelled of onions, of stew, laundry soap or engines, of pipe tobacco, lime blossom or road dust, of the fierce sweat of summer toil, but they all smelled unobtrusively; they smelled of nothing.

He raised his eyes and looked across the aisle, letting his glance rest where those who had received absolution were kneeling and saying their prayers of penance. Over there it smelled of Saturday, of peace, bath water, poppyseed rolls, of new tennis balls, like the ones his sisters bought on Saturdays with their pocket money, it smelled of the clear, pure oil Father cleaned his pistol with on Saturdays: it was black, his pistol, shining, unused for ten years, an immaculate souvenir of the war, discreet, useless; it merely served Father's memory, summoned a glow to his face when he took it apart and cleaned it; the glow of an erstwhile mastery over death, which a light touch on a spring could move out of the pale, gleaming magazine into the barrel. Once a week on Saturday, before he went to the club, this ritual of taking apart, caressing, oiling the black sections which lay spread out on the blue cloth like those of a dissected animal: the rump, the great metal tongue of the trigger, the smaller innards, joints and screws. He was permitted

177

to look on, he would stand there spellbound, speechless before his father's enraptured face; he was witnessing the celebration of the cult of an instrument which so frankly and terrifyingly resembled his sex; the seed of death was thrust out of the magazine. Father checked that too: to see whether the magazine springs were still working. They were still working, and the safety catch held back the seed of death in the barrel; with the thumb, with a tiny delicate movement, it could be released, but Father never released it; delicately his fingers fitted the separate parts together again before hiding the pistol under some old checkbooks and ledger sheets.

"It's your turn." He gestured again. Whispers. Whispered replies. The obtrusive smell of nothing.

Here on this side of the aisle it smelled of damnation, sins, the sticky banality of the other days of the week, the worst of which was Sunday: boredom, while the coffee percolator hummed on the terrace. Boredom in church, in the outdoor restaurant, in the boathouse, movie or café, boredom up at the vineyards where the progress of the Zischbrunner Mönchsgarten vines was inspected, slender fingers smoothly and expertly feeling the grapes; boredom which seemed to offer no escape except sin. It was visible everywhere: green, red, brown leather of handbags. Over there in the center nave he saw the rust-colored coat of the woman he had allowed to go ahead of him. He saw her profile, the delicate nose, the light brown skin, the dark mouth, saw her wedding ring, the high heels, those fragile instruments which harbored the deadly refrain: he listened to them going away, a long, long walk on hard asphalt, then on rough cobblestones: the crisp yet firm staccato of sin. Death, he thought, mortal sin.

Now she was actually leaving: she snapped her handbag shut, stood up, genuflected, crossed herself, and her legs passed on the rhythm to her shoes, her shoes to her heels, her heels to the tiles.

The aisle seemed to him like a river which he would never cross: he would stand forever on the banks of sin. Only four steps separated him from the voice which could release and bind, only six to the center nave, where Saturday reigned, peace, absolution—but he took only two steps as far as the aisle, slowly at first, then he ran as if fleeing from a burning house.

As he pushed open the padded door, light and heat hit him too suddenly; for a few seconds he was dazzled, his left hand struck the doorpost, the prayer book fell to the floor, he felt a jab of pain on the back of his hand, bent down, picked up the book, let the door swing back and stopped for a moment in the porch to smooth out the crumpled page of the prayer book. "Utter repentance," he read, before shutting the book; he put it into his trouser pocket, rubbed his smarting left hand with his right, and cautiously opened the door by pushing against it with his knee: the woman was no longer in sight, the forecourt was empty, dust lay on the dark green leaves of the chestnuts; near the lamppost stood a white ice-cream cart, from the lamppost hook hung a gray sack containing evening papers. The ice-cream man was sitting on the curb reading the evening paper, the news-paper vendor was perched on one of the shafts of the ice-cream cart licking an ice-cream cone. A passing street-car was almost empty: there was only a boy standing on the back platform, letting his green swimming trunks flap in the air.

Slowly Paul pushed open the door, went down the steps; within a few seconds he was sweating, it was too hot and too dazzling, and he longed for darkness.

There were some days when he hated everything ex-cept himself, but today was like most days, when he hated only himself and loved everything: the open win-dows in the houses around the square; white curtains, the clink of coffee cups, men's laughter, blue cigar smoke puffed out by someone he could not see; thick blue clouds came out of the window over the savings bank; whiter than fresh snow was the cream on a piece of cake which a girl standing at the window next door to the pharmacy was holding; white, too, was the ring of cream around her mouth.

The clock over the savings bank showed half past five.

Paul hesitated a moment when he reached the ice-cream cart, a moment too long, so that the ice-cream man got up from the curb, folded the evening paper, and Paul could read the first line on the front page: "Khru-shchev," and in the second line: "open grave"; he walked on, the man unfolded the paper and with a shake of his head sat down again on the curb.

When Paul had passed the corner by the savings bank and turned the next corner, he could hear a voice down on the riverbank announcing the next regatta race: men's four—Ubia, Rhenus, Zischbrunn 67. It seemed to Paul that he could smell and hear the river, which was a quarter of a mile away: oil and algae, the bitter smoke of the tugs, the slapping of the waves as the paddle steamers moved downstream, the hooting of long-drawn-out sirens in the evening; lanterns in outdoor cafés, chairs so red they seemed to burn like flames in the shrubberies.

He heard the starting gun, shouts, voices chanting, at first clearly in time with the beat of the oars: "Zisch-brunn, Rhe-nuss, U-bja," and then all mixed up: "Rhe-brunn, Zisch-nuss, Bja-Zisch-U-nuss."

Quarter past seven, thought Paul, till quarter past seven the town will stay as deserted as it is now. There were parked cars all the way to here, empty, hot, smelling of oil and sun, parked under trees, on both sides of the street, in driveways. As he turned the next corner and had a view of the river and the hills, he saw the parked cars up on the slopes, in the schoolyard, they were even parked in the entrances to the vineyards. In the silent streets through which he was walking they were parked on both sides, they heightened the impression of loneliness; he felt a pang at the glittering beauty of the cars, shining elegance from which the owners seemed to protect themselves with hideous mascots: grotesque monkey faces, grinning hedgehogs, distorted zebras with bared teeth, dwarfs leering malevolently above tawny beards.

The chanting became clearer, the shouts louder, then the announcer's voice proclaimed the victory of the

Zischbrunn four. Applause, fanfare, then the song: "Zischbrunn, high on the slopes, caressed by the river, nourished by wine, pampered by lovely women. . . ." Trumpets puffed out the tedious tune like soap bubbles into the air.

As he passed through a gateway it was suddenly quiet. In this courtyard behind the Griffduhnes' house the sounds from the river were muted: filtered through the trees, caught by old sheds, swallowed up by walls, the announcer's voice was subdued: "Ladies' pairs." The starting gun sounded like the pop from a toy pistol, the chanting like school choir practice behind walls.

Now his sisters were thrusting their oars into the water, their broad faces serious, beads of sweat forming on their upper lips, their yellow headbands turning dark; now their mother was adjusting the binoculars, elbowing away Father's hands which were trying to snatch the binoculars. "Zisch-Zisch-Brunn-Brunn" roared one chorus which drowned out the others, now and again a feeble syllable: "U-nuss, Rhe-bja," then a roaring that here in the courtyard sounded as if it came from a muffled radio. The Zischbrunn pair had won: now the sisters' faces relaxed, they tore off the sweat-darkened headbands, paddled calmly toward the judges' boat, waved to their parents. "Zisch-Zisch," shouted their friends, "Hurrah for Zisch!"

Over their tennis balls, thought Paul, red blood over the white fleecy balls.

"Griff," he called softly, "are you up there?"

"Yes," replied a languid voice, "come on up!"

The wooden staircase was saturated with summer heat, it smelled of tar, of ropes that had not been sold for the past twenty years. Griff's grandfather had owned all these sheds, buildings and walls. Griff's father owned scarcely a tenth of them, and: "As for me," Griff always said, "all I'll ever own will be the pigeon loft where Dad used to keep pigeons. You can stretch out comfortably in it, and I shall stay up there and contemplate my big right toe—but even the pigeon loft will only be mine because nobody wants it any more."

The walls upstairs were covered with old photographs. They were dark red, mahogany almost, the white had gone cloudy and yellow: picnics of the nineties, regattas of the twenties, lieutenants of the forties; young girls who had died thirty years ago as grandmothers looked soulfully across the passage at their life partners: wine merchants, rope chandlers, shipyard owners, whose Victorian melancholy had been captured and preserved by Daguerre's early disciples; a student of the year 1910 solemnly contemplated his son, an ensign who had frozen to death near Lake Peipus in Russia. Old furniture cluttered up the passage, and there was a stylish bookcase containing fruit jars, empty ones with limp red rubber rings rolled up on the bottom, full ones whose contents were only visible here and there through the dust; dark plum jam, or cherries of anemic red, pallid as the lips of sickly young girls.

Griffduhne was lying on the bed, naked from the waist up; his white, narrow chest contrasted alarmingly with his red cheeks: he looked like a poppy whose stalk has already withered. An unbleached linen sheet hung in front of the window, there were spots on it as if it were being X-rayed by the sun; the sunlight, filtered down to a yellow dusk, penetrated the room. Schoolbooks lay on the floor, a pair of slacks hung over the bedside table, Griff's shirt over the washbasin; a green corduroy jacket hung on a nail on the wall between the crucifix and photos of Italy: donkeys, steep cliffs, cardinals. An open jar of plum jam with a kitchen spoon sticking in it stood on the floor beside the bed.

"So they're rowing again; rowing, paddling, water sports—those are their problems. Dancing, tennis, wine harvest festivals, graduation parties. Songs. Is the town hall going to have gold, silver or copper columns? Don't tell me, Paul," he said, lowering his voice, "that you were actually down there?"

"I was."

"Well?"

"Nothing, I left again. I couldn't stand it. It's so pointless. How about you?"

"I haven't been for ages. What's the use? I've been thinking about what's the right height for our age: I'm too tall for fourteen, so they say, you're too short for fourteen. D'you know anyone who is just the right height?"

"Plokamm is the right height."

"Huh—d'you want to be like him?"

"No."

"You see," said Griff, "there are . . ." He hesitated,

broke off, as he watched Paul's eyes looking intently and uneasily around the room. "What's up? Are you looking for something?"

"Yes," said Paul, "where have you put it?"

"The pistol?"

"Yes, let me have it." Over the box with the new tennis balls is where I'll do it, he thought. "Come on," he said loudly, "hand it over."

"Wait," said Griff, shaking his head. Embarrassed he took the spoon out of the plum jam, then stuck it back in the jar, folded his hands. "No, let's smoke instead. There's lots of time before quarter past seven. Rowing, paddling, maybe it'll be even later. Outdoor reception. Lanterns. Prize-giving ceremony. Your sisters won the pairs. Zisch, zisch zisch . . . ," he went under his breath.

"Show me the pistol."

"Hell, why should I?" Griff sat up, seized the jar and threw it against the wall: broken glass flew, the spoon struck the edge of the bookshelf, from there it did a somersault in front of the bed. The jam splashed onto a book which said "Algebra I," some of it ran in a viscous blue across the yellow of the wall, dying it a kind of green. Without moving, without saying a word, the boys looked at the wall. When the noise of the crash had died away, and the last of the pulp had trickled down, they looked at each other in amazement: the shattering of the glass had left them unmoved.

"No," said Paul, "that's no good. The pistol's better, or maybe fire, a blaze or water—the pistol's best. Kill."

"But who?" asked the boy on the bed; he leaned over, picked up the spoon, licked it, and placed it tenderly on the bedside table.

"But who?"

"Me," said Paul hoarsely, "tennis balls."

"Tennis balls?"

"Oh nothing, give it to me. Now."

"Right," said Griff. He stripped off the sheet, jumped out of bed, kicked the broken glass aside, and took a narrow brown cardboard box from the bookshelf. The box was not much bigger than a pack of cigarettes.

"What?" said Paul. "Is that it? In there?"

"Yes," said Griff, "that's it."

"And that's what you fired eight shots at a tin can with, at a distance of thirty yards, and got seven hits?"

"That's right, seven," said Griff uncertainly, "don't you want to look at it even?"

"No I don't," said Paul; he looked angrily at the box, which smelled of sawdust, of the stuff blanks were packed in. "No I don't, I don't want to look at it. Show me the ammunition."

Griff bent down. From his long, pale back the vertebrae stood out, disappeared again, and this time he quickly opened the box, which was as big as a matchbox. Paul took one of the copper cartridges, held it between two fingertips, as if to see how long it was, turned it this way and that, shook his head as he contemplated the round, blue head of the bullet. "No," he said, "that's no good. My dad has one—I'll get my dad's."

"But it's locked up," said Griff.

"I'll get hold of it. As long as I do it before half past seven. He always cleans it then, before he goes to the club, he takes it apart: it's a big one, black and smooth, heavy, and the bullets are big like this"—he showed how big with his fingers—"and ..." He was silent, and sighed: over the tennis balls, he was thinking.

"Do you really want to shoot yourself, properly?"

"Maybe," said Paul. The feet of my eyes are sore, the hands of my eyes are sick, he thought. "Hell, you know how it is."

Griff's face suddenly turned dark and stiff; he swallowed, went to the door, only a few steps away; there he stopped.

"You're my friend," he said, "or aren't you?"

"Sure."

"Then go and get a jar too and throw it against the wall. Will you?"

"Why?"

"My mother," said Griff, "my mother told me she wants to have a look at my room when she gets back from the regatta, she wants to see whether I've improved. Tidied up and all that. She got mad at my report. Let her look at my room then—are you going to get the jar now?"

Paul nodded, went out into the passage and heard Griff call out: "Take the golden plum jam, if there's any left. Something yellow would look good, better than this purplish mess." Paul wiped off some of the jars outside in the semi-darkness till he found a yellow one. They won't understand, he thought, nobody will understand, but I have to do it; he went back to the room, raised his right hand and threw the jar against the wall.

"It's no good," he said quietly, while they both regarded the effect of the throw, "it's not what I want."

"What is it you want?"

"I want to destroy something," said Paul, "but not jars, or trees, or houses—and I don't want your mother to get mad, or mine; I love my mother, yours too—there's no sense to it."

Griff fell back onto the bed, covered his face with his hands and murmured: "Kuffang has gone to that girl."

"The Prohlig girl?"

"Yes."

"I've been with her too."

"You have?"

"Yes. She's not serious. Giggles around there in the passage—stupid, she's stupid. She doesn't know it's a sin."

"Kuffang says it's great."

"No, I tell you, it's not great. Kuffang's stupid too, you know he's stupid."

"I know he is, but what are you going to do?"

"Nothing with girls—they giggle. I've tried it. They're not serious—they just giggle." He went across to the wall and smeared his forefinger through the big splash of golden plum jam.

"No," he said without turning round, "I'm going to get my dad's pistol."

Over the tennis balls, he thought. They're as white as washed lambs. The blood over the lambs.

"Women," he whispered, "not girls."

The filtered noise of the regatta came faintly into the room. Men's eights. Zischbrunn. This time Rhenus won. The jam dried slowly on the wooden wall, became as hard as cow dung, flies buzzed around the room, there was a sweetish smell, flies crawled over the schoolbooks, the clothes, flew greedily from one spot, from one pool, to another, too greedy to stay long on one pool. The two boys did not move. Griff lay on the bed, staring at the ceiling and smoking. Paul perched on the edge of the bed, bent forward like an old man; deep within him, over him, on him, lay a burden to which he couldn't put a name, a dark heavy burden. Suddenly he stood up, ran out into the passage, snatched up one of the fruit jars, came back into the room, raised the jar—but he did not throw it; he stood there with the jar in his raised hand. Slowly his arm dropped, the boy put down the jar, on a paper bag which was lying neatly folded on the bookshelf. "Fürst Slacks," it said on the paper bag, "Fürst Slacks Are The Only Slacks."

"No," he said, "I'll go and get it."

Griff puffed his cigarette smoke at the flies, then aimed the butt at one of the pools. Flies flew up, settled hesitantly around the smoking butt, which sank slowly into the jam and fizzled out.

"Tomorrow evening," he said, "I'll be in Lübeck, at my uncle's; we'll go fishing, we'll sail and swim in the Baltic; and you, tomorrow you'll be in the Valley of the Thundering Hooves." Tomorrow, thought Paul, who did not move, tomorrow I shall be dead. Blood over the tennis balls, dark red like in the fleece of the lamb; the Lamb will drink my blood. O Lamb. I shall never see my sisters' little laurel wreath: "Winners of the Ladies' Pairs," black on gold; they'll hang it up there between the photos of holidays in Zalligkofen, between withered bunches of flowers and pictures of cats; next to the framed Graduation Diploma hanging over Rosa's bed, next to the certificate for long-distance swimming hanging over Franziska's bed; between the colored prints of their patron saints: Rosa of Lima, Franziska Romana; next to the other laurel wreath: "Winners of the Ladies' Doubles"; under the crucifix. The dark red blood will cling stiffly to the fuzz of the tennis balls, the blood of their brother who preferred death to sin.

"I must see it one day, the Valley of the Thundering Hooves," Griff was saying, "I must sit up there where you always sit, I must hear them, the horses charging up to the pass, galloping down to the lake, I must hear their hooves thundering in the narrow gorge—their whinnying cries streaming out over the mountain tops—like—like a thin fluid."

Paul looked disdainfully at Griff, who had sat up and was excitedly describing something he had never seen: horses, many horses, charging up over the pass, galloping with thundering hooves down into the valley. But there had only been *one* horse there, and only *once:* a colt which had raced out of the paddock and cantered down to the lake, and the sound of its hooves had not been like thunder, just a clatter, and it was such a long time ago, three years, maybe four.

"So you," he said quietly, "are going fishing; you'll go sailing and swimming, and stroll up the little streams, in wading boots, and catch fish with your hands."

"That's right," said Griff sleepily, "my uncle catches fish with his hands, even salmon, yes . . ." He sank back onto the bed with a sigh. His uncle in Lübeck had never caught a fish, not even with a rod or a net, and he, Griff, doubted whether there were any salmon at all up there on the Baltic and in the little streams. Uncle was just the owner of a small cannery; in old sheds in the back yard the fish were slit open, cleaned, salted or pickled; in oil or tomato sauce; they were pressed into cans by an ancient machine which threw itself with a grunt like a tired anvil onto the tiny cans and shut the fish up in tinplate. Lumps of damp salt lay around in the yard, fish bones and skin, scales and entrails, seagulls screamed, and light red blood splashed onto the white arms of the women workers and ran down their arms in watery trickles.

"Salmon," said Griff, "are smooth, silvery and pink, they're strong, much too beautiful to eat; when you hold them in your hand you can feel their strong muscles."

Paul shuddered: they had once had some canned salmon for Christmas, a putty-colored mass swimming in pink fluid, full of bits of fish bone.

"And you can catch them in the air when they jump," said Griff; he sat up, knelt on the bed, threw up his hands, fingers spread wide, brought them together till they looked as if they were about to strangle something; the rigid hands, the motionless face of the boy, it all seemed to belong to someone who worshiped a stern god. The soft yellow light bathed the rigid boyish hands, lent the flushed face a dark, brownish tinge—"Like that," Griff whispered, snatched with his hands at the fish that wasn't there, and suddenly dropped his hands, letting them hang limp, inert, by his sides. "Come on," he said, jumped off the bed, picked up the box with the pistol from the bookshelf, opened it before Paul could turn away, and held out the open bottom half of the box containing the pistol. "Look at it now," he said, "just have a look at it." The pistol looked rather pathetic, only the firmness of the material distinguished it from a toy pistol; it was even flatter, but the solidity of the nickel gave it some glamor and a degree of seriousness. Griffduhne threw the open box containing the pistol into Paul's lap, took the closed glass jar from the bookshelf, unscrewed the lid, separated the perished rubber ring from the edge, lifted the pistol out of the box, dropped it slowly into the jam; the boys watched while the level of the jam rose slightly, scarcely beyond the narrowing of the neck. Griff put the rubber ring back around the edge, screwed on the lid and replaced the jar on the bookshelf.

"Come on," he said, and his face was stern and dark again, "come on, we'll go and get your dad's pistol."

"You can't come with me," said Paul. "I have to climb in through a window because they didn't give me a key, I have to get in at the back. They would notice; they didn't give me a key because they thought I was going to the regatta."

"Rowing," said Griff, "water sports, that's all they

ever think about." He was silent, and they both listened
for sounds from the river: they could hear the cries of
the ice-cream vendors, music, fanfares, a steamer hooted.

"Intermission," said Griff. "Plenty of time still. All
right, go by yourself, but promise me you'll come back
with the pistol. Will you promise?"

"I promise."

"Shake."

They shook hands: they were warm and dry, and each
wished the other's hand had been firmer.

"How long will you be?"

"Twenty minutes," said Paul, "I've thought it out so
many times but never done it—with the screwdriver. It'll
take me twenty minutes."

"Right," said Griff, reached across the bed and took
his watch from the bedside table drawer. "It's ten to six,
you'll be back at quarter past."

"Quarter past," said Paul. He paused in the doorway,
looked at the great splashes on the wall: yellow and
purplish. Swarms of flies were sticking to the splashes,
but neither of the boys moved a finger to drive them
away. Laughter drifted up from the riverbank: the water
clowns had begun to add zest to the intermission. An
"Ah" rose up like a great soft sigh; the boys looked up
at the sheet over the window as if they expected it to billow out, but it hung limp, yellowish, the dirt spots were
darker now, the sun had moved farther westward.

"Water skiing," said Griff, "the women from the face
cream factory." An "Oh" came up from the river, a
sigh, and again the sheet did not billow out.

"The only one," said Griff quietly, "the only one who looks like a woman is the Mirzov girl." Paul did not move. "My mother," Griff said, "found the piece of paper with those things about the Mirzov girl on it—and her picture."

"Good God," said Paul, "d'you mean to say you had one too?"

"Yes," said Griff, "I spent all my pocket money on it—I—I don't know why I did it. I didn't even read what was on the paper, I stuck it in my report envelope, and my mother found it. D'you know what was on it?"

"No," said Paul, "I don't, I bet it's all lies, and I don't want to know about it. Everything Kuffang does is a lie. I'm off now—"

"Right," said Griff firmly, "hurry up and get the pistol, and come back. You promised. Go on, go."

"O.K.," said Paul, "I'm going." He waited a moment, listening to the sounds from the river: he could hear laughter, fanfare. "Funny I never thought of the Mirzov girl. . . ." And he said again: "O.K.," and went.

I I

Cutouts might be like that, she thought, miniatures or colored medallions: the images were sharply punched, round and clear, a whole series of them. She was looking at it from a distance of twelve hundred yards, magnified twelve times through binoculars: the church with the savings bank and pharmacy, in the center of the gray square an ice-cream cart: the first picture, detached and unreal; a section of the riverbank, above it, in a semicir-

cle of horizon, green water with boats on it, colored pennants: the second picture, the second miniature. The
series could be added to at will: hills with woods and a
monument; over there—what were their names?—
Rhenania and Germania, torch-bearing, stalwart female
figures with stern faces, on bronze pedestals, facing each
other; vineyards, with green vines—hatred welled up in
her, salty, bitter and satisfying: she hated wine; they
were always talking about wine, and everything they
did, sang or believed was associated ritually with wine:
puffy faces, mouths emitting sour breath, hoarse gaiety,
belching, shrill women, the bloated stupidity of the men
who thought they resembled this—what was he called?
—Bacchus. She hung onto this picture for a long time:
I'll certainly stick this little picture in my album of
memories, a round picture of a green vineyard with vines.
Perhaps, she thought, I might be able to believe in You,
their God, if it were not wine which turns into Your
blood for them, is wasted for them, poured out for those
useless idiots. My memory will be a clear one, as acid as
the grapes taste at this time of year when you pick one
the size of a pea. All the pictures were small, distinct
and ready to be stuck in; vignettes of sky-blue, grass-
green, river-green, banner-red, blending with the sounds
which formed the background to the pictures, as in a
movie, spoken words, dubbed-in music: chanting, hurrahs, shouts of victory, fanfare, laughter and the little
white boats, as tiny as the feathers of young birds, as
light too, and as quickly blown away, the white feathers
scudding airily across the green water; when they

breasts sometimes look on statues I don't like; the terrace: a garden umbrella, a table with a cloth and dirty cups and saucers, an empty wine bottle still with its white foil cap; oh Father, she thought, how wonderful to be going to you, and how wonderful that you don't drink wine, only schnapps.

Melting tar was dripping from the garage roof in a few places; then she jumped as Paul's face—eighty feet away, such a long way off, but in the binoculars only six feet—came directly toward her. His pale face looked as if he were on the verge of doing something desperate: he was blinking into the sun, his arms, fists clenched, were hanging down limply as if he were holding something, but he wasn't holding anything; his fists were empty, squeezed tight. He turned the corner of the garage, sweating, his breath labored, jumped up onto the terrace. The cups and saucers clinked on the table; he rattled at the door, took two steps to the left, swung himself up onto the windowsill and jumped into the room. The samovar gave off a silvery chime as Paul bumped into the buffet: inside, the rims of the glasses passed on the vibration to each other; they were still faintly twittering as the boy ran on, across the brass strip in the doorway; when he came to the tennis balls he paused, bent down, but did not touch them; he stood there for a long time, stretched out his hands again, almost as if in benediction or tenderness, suddenly pulled a little book out of his pocket, threw it on the floor, picked it up, kissed it and placed it on the shelf under the hall mirror; then all she could see was his legs as he ran upstairs, and in the center of this miniature was the carton with the tennis balls.

She sighed, lowered the binoculars, letting her eyes linger on the pattern of the carpet; it was rust-red, with a black pattern of innumerable squares all joined together in labyrinths, toward the middle of each labyrinth the red got thinner and thinner, the black wider and wider, almost dazzling in its purity.

His bedroom was in the front of the house, facing the street; she remembered it from the days when he had still been allowed to play with her: it must be a year or two ago now; she had been allowed to play with him till he had begun to stare at her breasts with such a strange persistence that it interfered with their game, and she had asked: What are you looking at, do you want to see it? and he had nodded as if in a dream; she had undone her blouse, and she did not realize it was wrong till it was already too late; she saw it was wrong, not from his eyes but from the eyes of his mother, who had been in the room all the time, who came over now and screamed, while the darkness in her eyes turned to stone—that scream, that's also something I have to preserve on one of the phonograph records of my memory; that's what the screams must have sounded like at the witch-burnings the man used to describe, the one who came to have discussions with Mother; he looked like a monk who no longer believes in God—and her mother looked like a nun who no longer believed in her God: home again in this place called Zischbrunn, after years of bitter disillusionment, salty error, preserved in the faith she had had and lost in something called Communism, floating in the brine of the memory of the man who was called Mirzov, drank schnapps, and had never possessed the faith which she had lost; her mother's words were as salty as her heart.

Scream across the carpet pattern, broken game on the floor: models of houses his father had been the sales agent for twenty years ago, little houses such as had not been built for twenty years; old pneumatic-post tubes from the bank, samples of rope which the other boy— that's right, Griff was his name—had contributed; corks of various sizes, various shapes; Griff had not been there that afternoon. All broken by that scream which was to hang over her in future like a curse: she was the girl who had done what one must never do.

As she sighed, her glance lingered on the rust-red carpet, watching the sparkling threshold for his brown shoes to reappear.

Languidly she swung the binoculars back to the table: under the garden umbrella on the terrace a basket of fruit, dark brown wickerwork full of orange peel, the wine bottle with the label: "Zischbrunner Mönchsgarten"; one still life after another, with an undercurrent of noise from the regatta; dirty plates with remains of ice cream; the folded evening paper, she could make out the second word in the headline: "Khrushchev," and in the second line: "open grave"; some cigarettes with brown filter tips, others white, stubbed out in the ashtray, a brochure from a refrigerator firm—but they had had one for ages!—a box of matches; russet mahogany, like fire in old paintings; the samovar gleaming on the buffet, silver and bright, unused for years, shining like some strange trophy. Teawagon with salt cellar and mustard pot, the big family photograph: the children sitting at table with their parents at a restaurant out in the country, in the background the pond with swans, then the waitress bringing the tray with two mugs of beer and three bottles of lemonade; in the foreground, the family seated at the table: on the right, in profile, their father, holding a fork level with his chest, a piece of meat skewered on it, noodles festooned round the meat, on the left their mother, a crumpled serviette in her left hand, a spoon in her right; in the middle the children, their heads below the edge of the waitress's tray: ice-cream dishes reached to their chins, patches of light, filtered through the leaves, lay on their cheeks; in the middle, framed by the curly heads of his sisters, the one who had stood for such a long time by the tennis balls and had then run upstairs: his brown shoes had still not returned across the brass strip.

The tennis balls again, on their right the clothes closet, straw hats, an umbrella, a linen bag with the handle of a shoebrush sticking out of it; in the mirror the large picture that hung in the hall on the left: a woman picking grapes, with eyes like grapes, a mouth like a grape.

Tired of looking, she put down the binoculars. Her eyes plunged across the lost distance, smarted; she closed them. Red and black circles danced behind her

closed lids, she opened them again, was startled to see
Paul coming through the door; he was carrying something which sparkled in the sun, and this time he did not
pause when he came to the tennis balls. Now that she saw
his face without the binoculars—detached from her collection of miniatures—now she was certain he was going
to do something desperate: once more the samovar
chimed, once more the glasses inside the buffet passed
along the vibration, twittering like women exchanging
secrets; Paul knelt down on the carpet in the corner by
the window. All she could see of him was his right elbow, moving back and forth like a piston, regularly disappearing in a forward drilling movement—she ran-
sacked her memory for a clue as to where she had seen
this movement, she imitated the drilling pumping movement and then she knew: he was holding a screwdriver.
The red-and-yellow checked shirt came, went, was still—
Paul jerked back a little; she saw his profile, raised the
binoculars to her eyes, was startled at the sudden nearness and looked into the open drawer; it contained bundles of blue checkbooks, neatly tied with white string,
and some ledger sheets, bound through the holes with
blue string; Paul hastily stacked up the bundles beside
him on the carpet, clutched something to his chest, something wrapped in a blue cloth, put it down on the floor,
replaced the checkbooks and ledger sheets in the drawer,
and again all she could see, while the bundle in the blue
cloth lay beside him, was the pumping drilling movement of his elbow.

She cried out when he unwrapped the cloth: black,

smooth, glistening with oil, the pistol lay in the hand that was much too small for it. It was as if the girl had shot her cry through the binoculars at him; he turned, she lowered the binoculars, screwed up her smarting eyes and called out: "Paul! Paul!"

He held the pistol close to his chest as he climbed slowly out of the window onto the terrace.

"Paul," she called, "come over here through the garden."

He put the pistol in his pocket, shaded his eyes with his hand, walked slowly down the steps, across the lawn, scuffed across the gravel by the fountain, dropped his hand when he suddenly found himself in the shadow of the summerhouse.

"Oh," he said, "it's you."

"Didn't you recognize my voice?"

"No—what d'you want?"

"I'm going away," she said.

"I'm going away too," he said, "so what? Everyone's going away, almost. I'm leaving tomorrow for Zallig-kofen."

"No," she said, "I'm leaving for good, I'm going to my father's in Vienna . . ." and she thought: Vienna, that has something to do with wine too, in songs anyway.

"Vienna," he said, "down there . . . and you're staying there?"

"Yes."

The look in his eyes, raised almost vertically to her, motionless, trance-like, frightened her: I am not your Jerusalem, she thought, no, I'm not, and yet your eyes have the look the eyes of pilgrims must have when they see the towers of their Holy City.

"I—" she said softly, "I saw everything."

He smiled. "Come on down," he said, "come on."

"I can't," she said, "my mother's locked me in, I'm not allowed out till the train leaves, but . . ." She suddenly stopped, her breathing was labored, shallow, excitement was choking her, and she said what she had not meant to say: "But why don't you come up here?"

I am not your Jerusalem, she thought, no, no; he did not lower his eyes as he asked: "How can I get up there?"

"If you climb up onto the roof of the summerhouse, I'll give you a hand and help you up onto the veranda."

"I—there's someone waiting for me," but he was already testing the trellis to see if it would hold; it had been recently nailed and painted, dense dark vineleaves were growing up the trellis, which formed a kind of ladder. The pistol swung heavily against his thighs; as he pulled himself up by the weather vane he remembered Griff, lying in his room back there, flies buzzing round him, with pale chest and red cheeks, and Paul thought of the little flat nickel pistol: I must ask Griff whether nickel oxidizes; if it does he'll have to stop them eating out of the jar.

The girl's hands were larger and firmer than Griff's hands, larger and firmer than his own too: he felt this and was ashamed when she helped him climb from the ridge of the summerhouse roof onto the veranda balustrade.

He brushed the dirt off his hands and said, without looking at the girl: "It's funny that I'm really up here."

"I'm glad you're here, I've been locked in since three." He looked warily over to her, at her hand, which was holding her coat together over her chest.

"Why've you got your coat on?"

"You know why."

"Because of that?"

"Yes."

He took a step toward her. "I expect you're glad to be going away?"

"Yes, I am."

"There was a boy in school this morning," he said in a low voice, "selling pieces of paper with things about you written on them, and a picture of you."

"I know," she said, "and he said I get part of the money he gets for the pieces of paper, and that he has seen me the way he drew me. None of it's true."

"I know it isn't," he said, "he's called Kuffang; he's stupid and tells lies, everyone knows that."

"But they believe him when he tells them *that*."

"Yes," he said, "it's strange, they do believe that."

She pulled her coat tighter around her chest. "That's why I have to leave so suddenly, quickly, before they all get back from the regatta—for a long time now they've given me no peace. You make a show of your body, they say; they say it when I wear a dress with a low neck, and they say it when I wear a dress with a high neck—and a sweater: they go crazy then—but I have to wear something, don't I?"

He watched her without emotion as she went on talking; he was thinking: funny that I never thought of her,
not once. Her hair was blond, her eyes seemed blond too,
they were the color of freshly planed beechwood: blond
and slightly moist.

"I don't make a show of my body at all," she said, "I
just have it."

He nodded, pushed the pistol up a bit with his right
hand, as it was lying heavy against his thigh. "Yes," he
said, and she was afraid: he had that dream face again:
you would have thought he was blind, that other time,
those empty, dark eyes had seemed to fall upon her and
yet past her in an unpredictable refraction, and now
again he looked as if he were blind.

"The man," she went on hurriedly, "who sometimes
comes to have discussions with my mother, the old man
with white hair, do you know him?" There was silence,
the noise from the river was too far off to disturb this
silence—"Do you know him?" she asked impatiently.

"Of course I know him," he said; "that's old Dulges."

"Yes, that's the one—he's looked at me like that
sometimes and said: Three hundred years ago they
would have burned you as a witch. A woman's hair
crackling, and the cry from a thousand unfeeling souls
unable to tolerate beauty."

"Why did you make me come up?" he asked. "To tell
me that?"

"Yes," she said, "and because I saw what you were
doing."

He pulled the pistol out of his pocket, held it up and

waited with a smile for her to scream, but she did not scream.

"What are you going to do with it?"

"I don't know, shoot at something."

"At what?"

"Maybe at me."

"Why?"

"Why?" he said. "Why? Sins, death. Mortal sin. Do you understand that?" Slowly, without touching her, he made his way past her, in through the open kitchen door, and leaned with a sigh against the cupboard; the picture was still there on the wall, the one he had not seen for so long, the one he thought about sometimes: factory chimneys, with red smoke rising up from them, smoke pouring out and joining together in the sky to form a blood-red cloud. The girl was standing in the doorway, turned toward him. There were shadows across her face, and she looked like a woman. "Come inside," he said, "they might see us; that would be bad for you, you know."

"In an hour," she said, "I shall be sitting in the train, here—here's my ticket: it's not a return." She held up the buff ticket, he nodded, and she put the ticket back in her coat pocket. "I shall take off my coat and be wearing a sweater, a sweater, d'you understand?"

He nodded again. "An hour's a long time. Do you know what sin is? Death. Mortal sin?"

"Once," she said, "the pharmacist wanted to—and the teacher too, your History teacher."

"Drönsch?"

"Yes, him—I know what they want; but I don't know

what their words mean. I know what sin is, too, but I don't understand it any more than I understand what the boys sometimes call out after me when I come home alone, in the dark; they call out after me from doorways, from windows, from cars sometimes, they called out things after me which I knew the meaning of but which I didn't understand. Do you know?"

"Yes."

"What is it?" she said. "Does it bother you terribly?"

"Yes," he said, "terribly."

"Even now?"

"Yes," he said, "doesn't it bother you?"

"No," she said, "it doesn't bother me—it just makes me unhappy that it's there and that other people want something—that they call out after me. Please tell me, why are you thinking of shooting yourself? Because of that?"

"Yes," he said, "simply because of that. Do you know what it means when it says in the Bible: Whatsoever thou shalt bind on earth shall be bound in heaven?"

"Yes, I know what that means; sometimes I stayed behind in class when they had Religion."

"Well then," he said, "maybe you also know what sin is. Death."

"I do," she said, "do you really believe all that?"

"Yes."

"Everything?"

"Everything."

"You know I don't believe it—but I do know that the worst sin of all is to shoot yourself—at least, that's what

I heard," she said, raising her voice, "with my own ears," she pulled her ear with her left hand, with her right she was still clutching her coat, "with my own ears I heard the priest say: We must not throw away the gift of life and toss it at God's feet."

"Gift of life," he said bitterly, "and God has no feet."

"Hasn't He?" she said quietly, "hasn't He any feet, didn't they pierce them?"

He was silent, then flushed and said in a low voice: "I know."

"Yes," she said, "if you really believe everything, the way you say you do, then you have to believe that too. Do you believe that?"

"What?"

"That we mustn't throw away the gift of life?"

"Oh I don't know," he said, and held the pistol straight up in the air.

"Come on," she said softly, "put it away. It looks so silly. Please put it away."

He placed the pistol in his right pocket, put his hand into his left pocket and took out the three cartridge clips. The metal clips lay without luster on the palm of his hand. "That should do," he said.

"Shoot at something else," she said, "for instance, at—" she turned round and looked back at his own home, through the open window. "At the tennis balls," she said.

A deep flush enveloped him like darkness, his hands went limp, the clips fell from his hand. "How did you know—?" he whispered.

"Know what?"

He bent down, picked up the clips from the floor, pushed one cartridge, which had dropped out, carefully back into the clip; he looked through the window at the house standing in full view in the sunshine: the tennis balls were lying back there white and hard in their carton.

Here, in this kitchen, it smelled of bath water, soap, of peace and fresh bread, of cake; red apples were lying on the table, a newspaper, and half a cucumber, its cut surface pale, green and watery; closer to the peel the cucumber flesh was darker and firmer.

"I also know," said the girl, "what they used to do to fight sin. I've heard about it."

"Who?"

"Those saints of yours. The priest told us about it: they whipped themselves, they fasted and prayed, not one killed himself." She turned toward the boy, afraid again: no, no, I'm not your Jerusalem.

"They weren't fourteen," said the boy, "or fifteen."

"Some of them must have been," she said.

"No," he said, "no, it's not true, most of them weren't converted till after they'd sinned." He came closer, pushing himself along the windowsill toward her.

"That's a lie," she said, "some of them didn't sin first at all—I don't believe any of that—if anything, I believe in the Mother of God."

"If *anything*," he said scornfully, "but She was the Mother of *God*."

He looked the girl full in the face, turned aside and

said in an undertone: "Forgive me ... yes, yes, I have tried. Prayed."

"And fasted?"

"Oh fasting," he said, "I don't care what I eat."

"That's not fasting. And whipping. I would do that, I would whip myself, if I believed."

"Doesn't it bother you really?" he whispered.

"No," she said, "it doesn't bother me, to *do* something, to see something, to say something—but it does bother you, doesn't it?"

"Yes, it does."

"What a pity," she said, "that you're so Catholic."

"Why a pity?"

"Otherwise I'd show you my breasts. I would like so much to show them to you—to you— Everyone talks about them, the boys call out things after me, but no one has ever seen them yet."

"No one?"

"No," she said, "no one."

"Show it to me," he said.

"It won't be the same as it was last time, you know when I mean."

"I know," he said.

"Was it terrible for you?"

"Only because Mother was so terrible. She was absolutely furious and told everyone about it. It wasn't so terrible for me. I would have forgotten all about it. Come here," he said.

Her hair felt smooth and hard; that surprised him, he

had thought it would be soft, but it was the way he imagined spun glass.

"Not here," she said; she pushed him along in front of her, slowly, for he did not let go of her head, he kept his eyes on her face while they moved, as if in some strange dance step invented by themselves, away from the open veranda door across the kitchen; he seemed to be standing on her feet, she seemed to be lifting him with every step.

She opened the kitchen door, pushed him slowly across the hall, opened the door to her room.

"Here," she said, "in my room, not out there."

"Mirzova," he whispered.

"Why do you call me that? My name is Mirzov, and Katharina."

"Everyone calls you that, and I can't think of you any other way. Show it to me now." He blushed, because again he had said "it" and not "them."

"It makes me sad," she said, "that for you it's a sin."

"I want to see it," he said.

"Not a soul—" she said, "you're not to talk to a soul about it."

"I won't."

"Promise?"

"I promise—but there's one person I must tell."

"Who's that?"

"Think for a moment," he said softly, "think for a minute, you should know all about that." She bit her lip, still clutching her coat tightly around her chest, looked thoughtfully at him and said: "Of course, you can tell him, but no one else."

"All right," he said, "now show it to me."

If she laughs or giggles, he thought, I'll shoot; but she did not laugh: she was so serious she was trembling, her hands fluttered as she tried to undo the buttons, her fingers were ice cold and stiff.

"Come here," he said gently, "I'll do it." His hands were calm, his fear lay deeper than hers; down in his ankles was where he felt it, they were like rubber and he thought he was going to fall over. He undid the buttons with his right hand, passed his left hand over the girl's hair, as if to comfort her.

Her tears came quite suddenly, silently, without warning, without fuss. They simply ran down her cheeks.

"Why are you crying?"

"I'm scared," she said, "aren't you?"

"Yes I am," he said, "I'm scared too." He was so nervous he almost tore off the last button, and he took a deep breath when he saw Mirzova's breasts; he had been scared because he was afraid of being disgusted, afraid of the moment when politeness would force him to pretend, so as to hide this disgust, but he was not disgusted and there was no need to hide anything. He sighed again. As suddenly as they had begun, the girl's tears stopped flowing. She held her breath as she looked at him: the least movement of his face, the expression in his eyes, she took in every detail, and she already knew that in years to come she would be grateful to him, because he had been the one to undo the buttons.

He looked at them closely, did not touch her, just shook his head, and laughter rose up in him.

"What is it?" she asked, "may I laugh too?"

"Go ahead, laugh," he said, and she laughed.

"It's beautiful," he said, and again he was ashamed because he had said "it" instead of "they," but he could not bring himself to say "they."

"Do it up again," she said.

"No," he said, "you do it up, but leave it for a moment." It was very quiet, the sun pierced the yellow curtains, which had dark green stripes. Dark stripes also lay across the faces of the children. You can't have a woman, thought the boy, at fourteen.

"Let me do it up," said the girl.

"All right," he said, "do it up," but he held her hands back for a moment, and the girl looked at him and laughed aloud.

"Why are you laughing now?"

"I'm so happy, aren't you?"

"Yes I am," he said, "I'm happy because it's so beautiful."

He let go her hands, stepped back and turned aside as she buttoned up her blouse.

He walked round the table, looked at the open suitcase lying on the bed; sweaters lay piled one on top of the other, underwear had been sorted into little heaps, the bed had already been stripped, the suitcase was lying on the blue mattress ticking.

"So you're really leaving?" he asked.

"Yes."

He moved on, looked into the open clothes closet: nothing but empty coathangers, a red hair ribbon dangling from one of them. He shut the closet doors, glanced over to the bookshelf above her bed: empty except for some used blotting paper, and a brochure standing at an angle against the wall: "All About Winegrowing."

When he looked around, her coat was lying on the floor. He picked it up, threw it on the table and ran out.

She was standing in the kitchen doorway, holding the binoculars. She winced when he laid his hand on her shoulder, lowered her binoculars, and gave him a frightened look.

"Please go," she said, "you must go now."

"Let me see it just once more."

"No, the regatta will be over soon, my mother's coming to take me to the train. You know what'll happen if anyone sees you here."

He said nothing, leaving his hand on her shoulder. She ran away quickly, round to the other side of the table, took a knife out of the drawer, cut off a piece of the cucumber, took a bite, put down the knife. "Please," she said, "if you stare at me like that much longer, you'll look like the pharmacist or that fellow Drönsch."

"Shut up," he said. She looked at him in astonishment as he suddenly came over to her, grasped her by the shoulder; she brought her hand up over his arm and put the piece of cucumber in her mouth and smiled. "Don't you understand," she said, "I was so happy."

He looked at the floor, let go her shoulder, went to the veranda, jumped onto the balustrade and called out:

"Give me a hand." She laughed, ran over to him, put down the piece of cucumber and held onto him with both hands, bracing herself against the wall while she slowly lowered him onto the roof of the summerhouse.

"I bet someone has seen us," he said.

"Probably," she said, "can I let go?"

"Not yet. When are you coming back from Vienna?"

"Soon," she said, "d'you want me to come soon?" He already had both feet on the roof and said: "You can let go now." But she did not let go, she laughed: "I'll come back. When d'you want me to come?"

"When I can look at it again."

"That might be a long time."

"How long?"

"I don't know," she said, looking at him thoughtfully. "First you looked as if you were dreaming, then all of a sudden you looked almost like the pharmacist; I don't want you to look like that and commit mortal sins and be bound."

"Let go now," he said, "or pull me up again."

She laughed, let go his hands, picked up the piece of cucumber from the balustrade and bit into it.

"I've got to shoot at something," he said.

"Don't shoot at anything living," she said, "shoot at tennis balls or at—at jam jars."

"What made you think of jam jars?"

"I don't know," she said, "I could imagine it might be fun to shoot at jam jars. It's bound to make a noise, and splash all over the place—wait a minute," she said hurriedly as he turned away and started to climb down; he turned back and looked at her gravely. "And, you know," she said softly, "you could stand at the railroad crossing, by the water tower, and fire into the air when my train goes by. I'll be looking out of the window and waving."

"Good," he said, "I'll do that, when does your train go?"

"Ten past seven," she said, "at seven-thirteen it passes the crossing."

"Then I'd better get going," he said, "good-by, you'll be back?"

"I'll be back," she said, "for sure." And she bit her lip and repeated under her breath: "I'll be back."

She watched him as he clung to the weather vane, till his feet had reached the trellis. He ran across the lawn, onto the terrace, climbed into the house, she saw him cross the brass strip again, pick up the carton of tennis balls, turn back, she heard the gravel crunching under his feet as, with the carton under his arm, he ran past the garage and out onto the street.

I hope he doesn't forget to turn round and wave, she thought. There he was, waving, at the corner of the garage, he pulled the pistol out of his pocket, pressed the barrel against the carton and waved once more before he ran round the corner and disappeared.

Up she went with the binoculars again, punching out circles of blue, medallions of sky; Rhenania and Germania, riverbank with regatta pennants, round horizon of river-green with shreds of banner-red.

My hair would crackle, she thought, it crackled even when he touched it. And in Vienna there's wine too.

Vineyard: pale green, sour grapes, leaves which those fat slobs tied around their bald heads to make them look like Bacchus.

She looked for the streets, the ones she could see into with the binoculars: the streets were deserted, all she could see was parked cars; the ice-cream cart was still there, she could not find the boy. I'll be—she thought with a smile, while she swept the binoculars toward the river again—I'll be your Jerusalem after all.

She did not turn round as her mother opened the front door and entered the hall. A quarter to seven already, she thought. I hope he makes it to the crossing by thirteen minutes after. She heard the suitcase being snapped shut and the tiny key being turned in the lock, heard the firm footsteps, and she winced as the coat fell over her shoulders: her mother's hands remained lying on her shoulders.

"Have you got the money?"

"Yes."

"Your ticket?"

"Yes."

"The sandwiches?"

"Yes."

"Did you pack your suitcase properly?"

"Yes."

"You haven't forgotten anything?"

"No."

"The address in Vienna?"

"Yes."

"The phone number?"

"Yes."

The brief pause was dark, frightening, her mother's hands slid down her shoulders, over her forearms. "I felt it was better not to be here during your last hours. It's easier that way, I know it is. I've said good-by so many times—and I did right to lock you in, you know."

"You did right, I know."

"Then come along now. . . ." She turned round; it was terrible to see her mother crying, it was almost as if a monument were crying: her mother was still beautiful, but it was a dark beauty, haggard. Her past hung over her like a black halo. Strange words echoed in the legend of Mother's life: Moscow—Communism—a Red nun, a Russian called Mirzov; her faith lost, escape, and the dogmas of the lost faith continuing to twist and turn in her brain; it was like a loom whose spools go on turning although there is no more yarn: gorgeous patterns woven into a void, only the sound remained, the mechanism; all she needed was an opposite pole: Dulges, the city fathers, the priest, the schoolteachers, the nuns; and if you shut your eyes you could imagine prayer wheels, the prayer wheels of the unbelieving, the restless wind-driven rattle known as discussion; occasionally, very rarely, her mother had looked the way she looked now: when she had been drinking wine, and people would say: Ah yes, in spite of everything she's still a true daughter of Zischbrunn.

It was a good thing her mother was smoking; trickling down toward the cigarette, wreathed in smoke, her tears looked less serious, more like pretended tears, but tears were the last thing her mother would pretend.

"I'll pay them back for this," she said. "I hate to see you go. To have to give in to them."

"Why don't you come too?"

"No, no—you'll be back, a year or two and you'll be back. Never do what they think you've been doing. Never, and now come along."

She slipped her arms into the sleeves of her coat, buttoned it up, felt for her ticket, for her purse, ran into her bedroom, but her mother shook her head as she went to pick up her suitcase. "Never mind that," she said, "and hurry—there's not much time."

Heat hung in the staircase, wine fumes rose from the cellar where the pharmacist had been bottling wine: an acrid smell which seemed to go with the hazy magenta of the wallpaper. The narrow lanes: the dark windows, doorways, from which things had been called out after her, things she did not understand. Hurry. The noise from the riverbank was louder now, car engines were being started up: the regatta was over. Hurry.

The ticket collector called her mother by her first name: "O.K., Kate, never mind about a platform ticket." A drunk staggered along the dark underpass, bawling out a tune, and hurled a full bottle of wine against the damp black wall; there was a crash of breaking glass, and once again the smell of wine rose to her nostrils. The train was already in, her mother pushed the suitcase into the corridor. "Never do what they think you've been doing, never."

How sensible to make the good-bys so short; there was only one minute left, it was long, longer than the whole afternoon. "I expect you'd have liked to take the binoculars along. Shall I send them on to you?"

"Yes, would you please? Oh Mother."

"What is it?"

"I hardly know him."

"Oh, he's nice, and he's looking forward to having you—and he never believed in the gods I believed in."

"And he doesn't drink wine?"

"He doesn't care for it—and he's got money, he's in business."

"What kind of business?"

"I don't know exactly: clothing, or something. You'll like him."

No kiss. Monuments must not be kissed, even when they weep. Without a backward glance her mother disappeared into the underpass: a pillar of salt, a monument to unhappiness, preserved in the bitter brine of her mistakes; that evening she would start up the prayer wheel, give a monologue while Dulges sat in the kitchen: "Aren't tears actually a remnant of bourgeois sentiment? Can there be tears in the classless society?"

Past the school, the swimming pool, under the little bridge, the long, long wall of the vineyards, the woods

—and at the railroad crossing by the water tower she saw the two boys, heard the bang, saw the black pistol in Paul's hand and shouted: "Jerusalem, Jerusalem!" and she shouted it again although she could no longer see the boys. She wiped away her tears with her sleeve, picked up her suitcase and stumbled along the corridor. I won't take off my coat yet, she thought, not just yet.

III

"What was it she called out?" asked Griff.

"Couldn't you hear?"

"No, could you? What was it?"

"Jerusalem," said Paul quietly. "Jerusalem, she shouted it again when the train had already gone by. Let's go." He looked disappointedly at the pistol, which he held in his lowered hand, his thumb on the safety catch. He had thought it would make more of a bang, that it would smoke; he had counted on it smoking: with a smoking pistol in his hand, that's how he had wanted to stand beside the train, but the pistol did not smoke, it was not even hot, he moved his forefinger carefully along the barrel, withdrew it. "Let's go," he said. Jerusalem, he thought, I could hear it quite plainly, but I don't know what it means.

They left the path that ran parallel to the railway tracks, Griff hugging under his arm the jar of jam he had brought from home, Paul carrying the pistol in his lowered hand; in the greenish light they turned to face each other.

"Are you really going to do it?"

"No," said Paul, "no, we must..." He blushed, turned his face away. "Did you put the balls on the tree trunk?"

"Yes," said Griff, "they kept rolling off, but then I found a groove in the bark."

"How far apart?"

"Four or five inches, like you said—listen," he said, lowering his voice and coming to a halt, "I can't go home, I can't. To that room. You do see, don't you, that I can't go back to that room." He moved the jam jar to his other hand, and held Paul, who wanted to go on, by the sleeve. "I just can't."

"No," said Paul, "I wouldn't go back to that room either."

"My mother would force me to clean it up. I can't, I tell you—wipe up the floor, clean the walls, the books, and everything. She would be standing there watching."

"No, you can't do that. Let's go!"

"What shall I do?"

"We'll see, let's shoot first, come along...." They walked on, from time to time turning their green faces toward one another, Griff nervously, Paul smiling.

"You've got to shoot me," said Griff, "you've got to, I tell you."

"You're crazy," said Paul; he bit his lip, raised the pistol, aimed at Griff, and Griff ducked, whimpered softly, and Paul said: "You see, you'd scream, and I haven't even moved the safety catch."

He shaded his eyes with his left hand when they reached the clearing, blinked across to the tennis balls which were lying in a row on a fallen tree: three were still spotless, white and fluffy, like the fleece of the Lamb, the others were muddy from falling on the damp ground.

"Go over there," said Paul, "put the jar between the third and fourth ball." Griff walked unsteadily across the clearing, placed the jar behind the balls so that it stood at an angle and threatened to topple over.

"There's not enough room, I can't put it in between."

"Out of my way," said Paul, "I'm going to shoot, stand over here by me."

He waited until Griff was standing beside him in the shade, raised the pistol, took aim, pressed the trigger, and, frightened by the echo of the first bullet, he banged away till the magazine was empty—the echo of the last two shots came back clearly out of the forest long after he had stopped firing. The tennis balls were still there, not even the jam jar had been hit. It was quite silent, there was just a slight smell of powder—the boy was still standing there, the raised pistol in his hand, he stood there as if he would stay there forever. He was pale, the chill of disappointment flowed into his veins, and his ears rang with the clear echo that was no longer there: clear, staccato barking reverberated in his memory. He closed his eyes, opened them again: the tennis balls were still there, and not even the jam jar had been hit.

He pulled back his arm as if from a great distance, stroked his fingers along the barrel: at least it was a little hot. Paul ripped out the empty clip with his thumb nail, slid a new one in, and pushed the safety catch back.

"Here," he said quietly, "it's your turn."

He handed the pistol to Griff, showed him how to release the safety catch, stepped back and thought, while he stood in the shade trying to swallow his disappointment: I hope you don't miss, at least; I hope you don't miss. Griff threw up his arm with the pistol, then lowered it slowly toward the target—he's read about that, thought Paul, read that somewhere, it looks as though he had read it—and Griff fired stutteringly: once—then silence; there were the balls, and the jar was still standing there; then three times—and three times the echo yapped back at the two boys. The dark treetrunk lay there as peaceful as some strange still life, with its six tennis balls and the jar of plum jam.

Only an echo, there was a faint smell of powder, and, shaking his head, Griff handed the pistol back to Paul.

"I've got an extra shot coming to me," said Paul, "the one I fired in the air—that leaves two for each of us, and one left over."

This time he aimed carefully, but he knew he would miss, and he did miss: the echo of his shot came back to him thin and forlorn, the echo penetrated him like a red dot, circled around inside him, flew out of him again, and he was calm as he handed Griff the pistol.

Griff shook his head. "The targets are too small, we must pick bigger ones; how about the station clock or the Rapier Beer sign?"

"Where d'you mean?"

"At the corner, across from the station, where Drönsch lives."

"Or a windowpane, or the samovar we have at home. We've *got* to hit something. Is it really true that you fired eight times with your pistol and got seven hits? A tin can at thirty yards?"

"No," said Griff, "I didn't shoot at all, I've never shot before." He went over to the treetrunk, kicked the balls, the jam jar, with his right foot; the balls rolled into the grass, the jar slipped off and fell over onto the soft ground in the shade of the treetrunk where no grass grew. Griff snatched up the jar and was about to throw it against the tree, but Paul held back his arm, took the jar from him and put it on the ground. "Please, don't," he said, "don't—I can't bear to see it. Leave it where it is, let grass grow over it, lots of grass. . . ."

And he pictured the grass growing till the jar was completely covered; animals would sniff at it, mushrooms would grow in a dense colony, and years later he would go for a walk in the forest and find it: the pistol covered with rust, the jam decayed into a moldy, spongy scum. He took the jar, set it in a hollow at the edge of the clearing, and kicked some loose earth over it. "Leave it," he said softly, "leave the balls too—we haven't hit a thing."

"Lies," said Griff, "all lies."

"Yes, all lies," said Paul, but while he was fastening the safety catch and putting the pistol in his pocket he said under his breath: "Jerusalem, Jerusalem."

"How did you know she was leaving?"

"I met her mother on my way over to you."

"But she'll be back, won't she?"

"No, she won't be back."

Griff returned to the clearing, kicked the balls, two of them rolled white and silent into the shady forest. "Come over here," he said, "look at this, we aimed much too high."

Paul walked slowly across, saw the ragged blackberry bush, bullet holes in a fir tree, fresh resin, a snapped branch.

"Come on," he said, "let's shoot at the Rapier Beer sign, it's as big as a cartwheel."

"I'm not going back into town," said Griff, "never again, I'm going to Lübeck, I've got the ticket right here. I'm not coming back."

They walked slowly back the way they had come, past the railroad crossing, past the long vineyard wall, past the school. The parked cars had long since left, the sound of music drifted up from the town. They climbed up onto the two pillars of the churchyard gates, sat ten feet apart at the same level and smoked.

"Prize-giving ceremony," said Griff. "A ball. Vine leaves round their foreheads. Down there you can see the Rapier Beer sign on the wall of Drönsch's house."

"I'll hit it," said Paul, "aren't you coming?"

"No, I'll stay here, I'm going to sit here and wait till you've shot it down. Then I'll walk slowly over to Dreschenbrunn, get on the train there and go to Lübeck. I'll go for a swim, a long swim in the salt water, and I hope it'll be stormy, with high waves and lots of salt water."

They smoked silently, looked at each other now and

then, smiled, listened to the sounds coming up from the town which were getting louder and louder.

"Did the hooves really thunder?" asked Griff.

"No," said Paul, "they didn't, it was only one horse, and his hooves just clattered—how about the salmon?"

"I've never seen one." They exchanged smiles and were silent for a while.

"Now my dad's standing in front of the cupboard," Paul said then, "with his shirtsleeves rolled up, my mother's spreading the tablecloth; now he's unlocking the drawer; perhaps he can see the scratch I made when the screwdriver slipped; but he doesn't see it, it's dark now over there in the corner; he's opening the drawer, he stops in surprise, for the checkbooks and ledger sheets aren't lying the way he left them—he's got the wind up, he's calling out to my mother, he's throwing all the stuff on the floor, rummaging around in the drawer—now, right now—at this very moment." He looked at the church clock, whose big hand was just slipping onto the ten while the small one stood motionless below the eight. "At one time," said Paul, "he was champion pistol-cleaner in his division; in three minutes he could take a pistol apart, clean it, and put it together again—and at home I always had to stand beside him and check the time with a stop watch: it never took him more than three minutes."

He threw his cigarette butt onto the path, stared at the church clock. "At exactly ten to eight he was always through with the job, then he would wash his hands and still be at the club on the stroke of eight." Paul jumped down from the pillar, held his hand up to Griff and said: "When'll I see you again?"

"Not for a long time," said Griff, "but one day I'll be back. I'll go to work for my uncle, canning fish, slitting them open—the girls are always laughing, and in the evening they go to the movies, maybe—they don't giggle, that's for sure. They've got such white arms and look so cute. They used to stuff chocolate in my mouth when I was little, but now I'm not so little any more. I can't—" he said quietly, "you do see, don't you, that I can't go back to that room. She would stand beside me till it was all cleaned up. Have you got any money?"

"Sure, I've got all my vacation money already. Do you want some?"

"Yes, let me have some, I'll send it back to you, later on."

Paul opened his wallet, counted out the coins, opened the flap for the bills. "All my money for Zalligkofen, I can let you have eighteen marks. D'you want it?"

"Yes," said Griff; he took the bill, the coins, stuck it all in his trouser pocket. "I'll wait here," he said, "till I can hear and see that you've shot down the Rapier Beer sign; fire quickly and empty the whole magazine. When I can hear it, and see it, I'll go over to Dreschenbrunn and get on the next train. But don't tell anyone you know where I've gone."

"I won't," said Paul; he ran off, kicking stones aside as he ran, letting out a shrill cry so as to hear the wild echo of his voice as he ran through the underpass; he did not slow down until he was passing the railway yard and approaching Drönsch's house; he gradually slackened speed, turned round but could not see the churchyard gates yet, only the big black cross in the middle of the churchyard and the white gravestones above the cross; the closer he came to the station, the more rows of graves he could see below the cross: two rows, three, five, then the gates, and Griff was still sitting there. Paul crossed the station square, slowly; his heart was thumping, but he knew it was not fear, it was more like joy, and he would have liked to fire off the whole magazine into the air and shout "Jerusalem"; he felt almost sorry for the big round Rapier Beer sign, on which two crossed swords seemed to protect a mug overflowing with foaming beer.

I must hit it, he thought, before taking the pistol out of his pocket, I must. He walked past the houses, stepped back into the doorway of a butcher's shop and nearly trod on the hands of a woman who was washing the tiled entrance. "Watch it, can't you?" she said out of the semi-darkness, "beat it!"

"Excuse me," he said, and took up a position outside the entrance. The soapsuds ran between his feet across the asphalt into the gutter. This is the best place, he thought, it's hanging directly in front of me, round, like a big moon, and I'm bound to hit it. He took the pistol out of his pocket, released the safety catch, and smiled, before he raised it and took aim: he no longer felt something had to be destroyed, and yet he had to shoot: there were some things that had to be done, and if he didn't shoot, Griff wouldn't go to Lübeck, wouldn't see the white arms of the cute girls, and would never go with one of them to the movies. He thought: God, I hope I'm not too far away—I *must* hit it, I *must;* but he had already hit it, the crash of the falling glass was almost louder than the noise of the shots. First a round piece broke out of the sign—the beer mug; then the swords fell, he saw the plaster of the house wall jump out in little clouds of dust, saw the metal ring which had held the glass sign, splinters of glass were clinging to the edge like a fringe.

Drowning out everything else were the screams of the woman; she had rushed out of the passageway and then run back and went on screaming inside in the dark—men were shouting too, a few people came out of the station; a great many rushed out of the tavern. A window was opened, and for a moment Drönsch's face appeared up above. But no one came near him because he was still holding the pistol. He looked up toward the churchyard: Griff had gone.

An eternity passed before someone came and took the pistol from him. He had time to think of many things: Now, he thought, Father has been yelling all over the house for the past ten minutes, putting the blame on Mother—Mother, who found out ages ago that I climbed up to Katharina's room; everyone knows about it, and nobody will understand why I did it and why I did this: shot at the lighted sign. Maybe it would have been better if I had shot into Drönsch's window. And he thought: Maybe I ought to go and confess, but they won't let me: it was eight o'clock, and after eight you couldn't confess.

The Lamb has not drunk my blood, he thought, O Lamb.

There are only a few pieces of broken glass, and I have seen Katharina's breasts. She'll come back. And for once Father has good reason to clean his pistol.

He even had time to think of Griff, now on his way to Dreschenbrunn, over the slopes, past the vineyards, and he thought of the tennis balls and the jar of jam, which he already imagined completely overgrown.

A lot of people were standing around him at some distance. Drönsch was leaning out of the window on his arms, his pipe in his mouth. Never will I look like that, he thought, never. Drönsch was always talking about Admiral Tirpitz. "Tirpitz was the victim of injustice. One day history will see that justice is done to Tirpitz. Objective scholars are at work to find out the truth about Tirpitz." Tirpitz? Oh well.

From behind, he thought, I might have known they would come from behind. Just before the policeman grabbed hold of him, he smelled his uniform: its first smell was of cleaning fluid, its second, furnace fumes, its third. . . .

"Where do you live, you young punk?" asked the policeman.

"Where do I live?" He looked at the policeman. He knew him, and the policeman must know him too: he always brought round the renewal for Father's gun license, a friendly soul, always refused a cigar three times before he accepted it. Even now he was not unfriendly, and his grasp was not tight.

"That's right, where do you live?"

"I live in the Valley of the Thundering Hooves," said Paul.

"That's not true," shouted the woman who had been scrubbing the passageway, "I know him, he's the son—"

"All right, all right," said the policeman, "I know. Come along," he said, "I'll take you home."

"I live in Jerusalem," said Paul.

"Now stop that," said the policeman, "come along with me."

"All right," said Paul, "I'll stop."

The people were silent as he walked down the dark street just ahead of the policeman. He looked like a blind man: his eyes fixed on a certain point, and yet he seemed to be looking past everything; he saw only one thing: the policeman's folded evening paper. And in the first line he could read: "Khrushchev" and in the second: "open grave."

"Hell," he said to the policeman, "you know where I live."

"Of course I do," said the policeman, "come along!"

The seventh trunk

For thirty-two years I have been trying to finish writing a story, the beginning of which I read in the *Bockelmunden Parish News* but the promised continuation of which I never got to see, since, for unknown reasons (probably political—it was in 1933) this modest publication ceased to appear. The name of the author of this story is engraved on my memory: he was called Jacob Maria Hermes, and for thirty-two years I have tried in vain to find other writings by him; no encyclopedia, no authors' society index, not even the Bockelmunden parish register, still extant, lists his name, and it looks as though I must finally accept the fact that the name of Jacob Maria Hermes was a pseudonym. The last editor of the *Bockelmunden Parish News* was Vice-Principal Ferdinand Schmitz (retired), but by the time I had finally tracked him down I was unduly delayed by prewar, wartime, and postwar events, and when at last in 1947 I trod my native soil again, I found that Ferdinand Schmitz had just died at the age of eighty-eight.

I freely admit that I invited myself to his funeral, not

only to do final honor to a man under whose editorship at least half of *the* most masterly short story I had ever read had been published; and not only because I hoped to find out more about Jacob Maria Hermes from his relatives—but also because in 1947 attendance at a country funeral meant the promise of a decent meal. Bockelmunden is a pretty village: old trees, shady slopes, half-timbered farmhouses. On this summer's day, tables had been set up in the yard of one of the farms, there was home-slaughtered meat from the Schmitz family storerooms, there was beer, cabbage, fruit, later on cakes and coffee—all served by two pretty waitresses from Nellessen's inn; the church choir sang the hymn that is *de rigueur* on the occasion of schoolteachers' funerals, "With wisdom and honor hast thou mastered the school." Trumpets sounded, club banners were unfurled (illegally, for this was still prohibited at that time); when the jokes grew broader, the atmosphere—as it is so nicely put—became more relaxed, I sat down beside each person there and asked them all in turn if they knew anything about the editorial estate of the deceased. The answers were unanimous and shattering: in five, six, or seven cartons (the information varied only as to quantity), the entire archives, the entire correspondence of the *Bockelmunden Parish News* had been burned during the final days of the war "as a result of enemy action."

Having eaten my fill and drunk a little too much, yet without obtaining any precise information on Jacob Maria Hermes, I returned home with that sense of dis-

chance that the printer and publisher were still to be found at this corner, and somehow I am quite touched at the thought of that thirteen-year-old boy immediately mounting his bicycle and racing from a westerly part of the city to that southerly one to discover that the two streets do not form a corner at all. To this day I admire the persistence with which I rode from the northern entrance of Römer Park, where at that time the built-up right-hand side of Maternus Street came to an end, to the Teutoburg Street, which had (and still has) the impudence to end shortly before the western entrance to Römer Park—from there to the office of the Tourist Association where with a pencil I furtively extended the right side of Maternus Street and the left side of Teutoburg Street on the city map hanging there, to discover that, if these two streets formed a corner, they would do so in the middle of the Rhine. So Heinrich Knecht, the old so-and-so, provided he was halfway honest, must have lived roughly fifty yards north of Marker 686 in a caisson at the bottom of the Rhine and have swum every morning a mile and a half down-river to report for duty at his Cuirassiers' barracks. *Today* I am no longer so certain that he really did not live there, perhaps still does: a deserter from the Cuirassiers, the color of the river, with a green beard, consoled by naiads—little knowing that for deserters times are still bad. *At the time* I was simply so shattered by all this hocus-pocus that I bought the first three cigarettes in my life with my last nickel; I enjoyed the first cigarette, and since then I have been a fairly heavy smoker. Needless to say, there was no trace either of the Nellessen printing shop. I did not even attempt to find Knecht—perhaps I ought to have got hold of a boat, dived in fifty yards north of Marker 686, and taken hold of Heinrich Knecht by his green beard. The thought never occurred to me at the time—*today* it is too late: I have smoked too many cigarettes since then to risk a dive, and Knecht is to blame for that.

I need hardly mention that I soon knew Knecht's treatise by heart; I carried it with me, on my person, in war and peace; during the war I lost it, it was in a haversack that also contained (I beg forgiveness of all militant atheists!) a New Testament, a volume of poems by Trakl, the half-story by Hermes, four blank furlough certificates, two spare paybooks, a company stamp, some bread, some *ersatz* spread, a package of fine-cut, and some cigarette paper. Cause of loss: enemy action.

Today, enriched, saturated almost, by literary insight and hindsight, and a little more perspicacious too, I have, of course, no difficulty in realizing that Knecht and Hermes must have known about each other, that both names were perhaps pseudonyms for Ferdinand Schmitz—that the name Nellessen linking the two should have put me on the track.

These are unpleasant, embarrassing assumptions, terrible consequences of an education that was forced upon me, betrayal of that earnest, flushed boy riding his bicycle right across Cologne that summer's day to find a street corner that did not exist. It was not until much later, actually only now that I am writing it down, that I realized that names, all names, are but sounding brass: Knecht, Hermes, Nellessen, Schmitz—and the only thing that matters is: someone actually wrote this half of a short story, actually wrote "The Seventh Trunk," so when I am asked to acknowledge who encouraged me to write, who influenced me, here are the names: Jacob Maria Hermes and Heinrich Knecht. Unfortunately I cannot reproduce the Hermes short story word for word, so I will merely relate what happened in it. The central character was a nine-year-old girl who, in a school playground surrounded by maple trees, was persuaded, duped, perhaps even forced, by a nun who in a nice way was not quite right in the head to join a brotherhood whose members undertook to attend Holy Mass on Sundays, "reverently," not once but twice. There was only one weak sentence in the story, and I can recall it—the weaknesses of one's fellow writers are always what one remembers best—word for word. The sentence goes: "Sister Adelheid suddenly became aware of her senselessness." First of all I am firmly convinced that there was a typographical error here, that instead of senselessness it should have been sensualness (in my own case it has happened three times that printers, typesetters, and proofreaders have made senselessness out of sensualness); secondly: an outright psychological statement of this kind was utterly out of keeping with Hermes' prose style, which was as dry as immortelles. In the preceding sentence a spot of cocoa on the little girl's blue blouse had been mentioned. He must have meant sensualness. I swear with even greater emphasis: a man of the stature of a Jacob Maria Hermes does not regard nuns as senseless, and nuns who become aware of their senselessness simply do not belong in his repertoire, especially as three paragraphs further on, in a prose as arid as the steppes, he let the little girl become fourteen years old without having her suffer complexes, conflicts, or convulsions, although usually she went only once to church, on many Sundays not at all, and only on a single occasion twice. Nowadays one does not have to even get wind of ecclesiastical wrath, one has only to be an ardent TV-viewer, to know that both terms, senselessness and sensualness, as applied to a nun, will find their way directly into the Church Council chamber and out again. For some Council fathers would immediately attack the term senselessness as applied by a nun in an internal monologue to her own existence; others would defend it; and needless to say it would not be the attackers but the defenders who would cause an author considerable trouble, for he would have to point to a printer's error, send them a notarized copy of his manuscript, and still they would interpret his allusion to a typographical error as cowardice and maintain that he was "attacking progress from the rear."

It stands to reason that it was not Hermes' intention to attack anything or anyone from the rear, or to turn his back on anyone or anything. I am so indebted to him that, in his place, I bare my breast to reactionaries and avant-gardists alike, because I know very well: a short story which speaks of a brotherhood whose members undertake to attend Mass not once but twice on Sundays —prose of this kind is highly suspect to both parties.

For thirty-two years now I have been carrying the end of this story around with me, and what rejoices me as a contemporary but inhibits me as an author is the fact that I know (no: I sense) that this woman is still alive, and perhaps this is why the seventh trunk will not spring open.

This is precisely the place where I must finally explain about Knecht's seventh trunk. Before doing so I must quickly, in a few sentences, deal with the numerous works of which none ranks equally with Knecht's but of which many are worthy of considerable note. It seems to me there are so many handbooks on how to write a short story that I am often surprised that not more good ones are written. For instance: the directions given in every creative writing course, teaching every beginner, clearly and to the point, with a minimum of fuss, how to make a story so attractive and so convenient that it poses not the slightest difficulty for the Sunday supplement copy editor—i.e., has a maximum length of one hundred column-length lines, in other words roughly the size (comparatively speaking, of course) of the smallest transistor in the world. And there are many more directions than those I have mentioned: one has only to read them *and then just simply* (these four expansion words contain the entire secret of short-story writing), and then just simply write it down, except—except that Knecht's very last injunction states: "And from the

stage, the "preparation of subject matter," as Knecht calls it, to put a railway station, or a school, a bridge over the Rhine, or a whole block of tenements? He has to rent an abandoned factory site until—and it may take years—he needs only the color of the bridge, only the smell of the school, and these he must put into the second trunk, although in this second trunk a horse, a truck, a barracks; and an abbey may be waiting, of which, as soon as it is the third trunk's turn, he will keep only a hair, a squeak, the echo of a command, and a response, while in the third trunk an old blanket, cigarette butts, empty bottles, and a few pawn tickets are waiting. Pawn tickets were evidently Knecht's favorite documents, for I recall a sentence of his: "Why, O Scribe, carry large objects around with you, when there are institutions which not only relieve you of having to store these objects but even give you money for them, money that you do not need to pay back if, after the due date, you are no longer interested in the object? Make use, therefore, of the institutions which help you to lighten your baggage." It does not take long to tell all the rest, for all the rest consists of: and so on. Needless to say—I am most anxious to avoid any misunderstanding—needless to say, the fifth or sixth trunk can be some little container the size of a matchbox, and the seventh can be an old biscuit tin; all that matters is that the seventh trunk must be closed, if only by a plain rubber band, and it must spring open by itself. Only one question remains unresolved, and it will probably cause youthful readers some anxiety: what does one do with living people where they are needed for short prose? One can neither—and possibly for twenty years, for it can take a good short story that long to wait for its awakening in the seventh trunk—so, one cannot shut living people up for that long, nor can one leave them at the pawnbroker's; what is one to do with them? Answer: they are not needed: one can pull out a hair, secretly remove a shoelace from a shoe, or brush a lipstick across a piece of cigarette paper; that is enough, for—here I must earnestly remind readers of my great-grandmother Nellessen: the point is not to put life into the case or box, the point is that life has to be created in it and jump out of its own accord. And so on—*and then just simply write* the whole thing *down.*

About the Author

HEINRICH BÖLL is one of postwar Germany's best known and most significant novelists and short story writers. Several of his books, among them *Acquainted with the Night, Adam, Where Art Thou?, Tomorrow and Yesterday, Billiards at Half-past Nine, Absent without Leave,* and *The Clown,* have been published in the United States and received critical acclaim. *The Clown* was chosen by the American Library Association for its Distinguished Books List of 1965. Born in 1917, Mr. Böll was drafted into the German Army during World War II and was wounded. He fought on several fronts, including the Russian, before being captured and repatriated. In his eloquent rejection of the senselessness of war and the hypocrisy of modern life, his affirmation of the poetry of human experience, his sense of sin and lust and death, he has become one of the most vital voices in the new Germany and in European literature. Heinrich Böll is rapidly growing in stature and recognition in America, and this brilliant collection of stories can only further distinguish him.

Catalog

If you are interested in a list of fine Paperback
books, covering a wide range of subjects
and interests, send your name and address,
requesting your free catalog, to:

McGraw-Hill Paperbacks
1221 Avenue of Americas
New York, N.Y. 10020